IN THE MIDST OF WOLVES

IN THE MIDST OF WOLVES

Barry McGuire
and
Logan White

CROSSWAY BOOKS • WHEATON, ILLINOIS
A DIVISION OF GOOD NEWS PUBLISHERS

In the Midst of Wolves.

Published by Crossway Books, a division of
Good News Publishers, Wheaton, Illinois 60187.

Cover illustration: David Yorke

Cover typography: Jim Lee

First printing, 1990

Printed in the United States of America

Library of Congress Cataloging in Publication Data

McGuire, Barry, 1935-
    In the midst of Wolves / Barry McGuire
        p.   cm.
    ISBN 0-89107-572-0 : $9.95
    I. White, Logan, 1948-   . II. Title
PS3563.C368181S   1990
813'.54--dc20

90-80612
CIP

To Mari and Stephanie,
who never stopped believing

CONTENTS

"Behold, I send you therefore as sheep in the midst of wolves; be ye, therefore, wise as serpents and harmless as doves."

(Matthew 10:16)

THE FESTIVAL
SUMMER, 1969

*T*he newscopter banked and turned, a muffled chopping in the hot Texas sky. It dangled over the dancing mobs and caused Clint Backer to glance upward.

As he squinted into the glare, mounds of cartilage made heaps and valleys around the bridge of a nose that had been shattered years before in a Waco bar, the name of which he no longer remembered, in a battle over a woman whose face he had forgotten.

Snub-nosed shade from the copter passed over him, momentarily hiding the network of purple-white scars that covered his bare arms and chest.

But the insignia on the back of his leather vest was still plainly visible: the sign of a snarling wolf's-head, and one word beneath it.

Wolves.

"They keep coming and coming," the girl beside the copter pilot said into her headset as the chopper floated lower. "It looks as if the entire generation wants to perpetuate the Summer of Love with this FaveRock Productions concert in a makeshift camp outside Galveston."

Turning away from the noise in the sky, Clint peered through waves of heat shimmering over the crowd. His long, lank brown hair was pulled tightly back under a black bandanna, but the sweat trickled into his eyes anyway.

At the bandstand—behind the concert promoter Aubrey Favereu—slouched a shadow belonging to his friend Roper, silent and solemn as a tombstone. Next to Roper, the object of Backer's search, was his younger brother, Colt.

Colt's head was thrown back, and his throat quivered in a wild and wicked laugh, enhanced, Clint knew, by the Methedrine injected through the countless pinpricks that ran over his lean arms, marks he kept covered by the leather Wolves jacket he wore even in this furnace-festival.

With an anxiety become chronic, Backer shoved his way through the mob, toward his brother Colt.

While he struggled, unholy feedback squeal hit his face as the band stopped and microphones were aimed at the skinny figure of Aubrey Favereu, perspiration soaking through the white of his cuffs and collar and the yellow paisley of his shirt.

The tail of a reporter's question snapped through the speakers at Backer as he neared the stand.

". . . your private army, allegedly responsible for the sudden flood of drugs that began last night after your gang howled into camp at sundown, like a band of motorized banshees."

Favereu leaned into the spray of microphones. "The Wolves are paid, professional peacekeepers—two hundred of 'em."

A smile spread across the promoter's pockmarked face, beneath his wrap-around lenses which reflected back the images of minicams nibbling away at his paisley image.

"This is just love happening, man. There ain't nothing else."

A girl with hair the color of dirty honey took the stage as Favereu faded away. Keyboards screamed, and her sound covered the camp.

Brushing up against Clint Backer was a thickset girl with dark eyes and a loose mouth. She danced into him, but Backer picked her up, set her aside, and moved toward the stage.

There were shouts, and a space opened up before him as two bare-chested men, one swinging six inches of knife-steel, circled each other, long hair sticking against their bare backs.

"You're dealin' nothin' but speed cut with—" the knife-wielder shouted, lunging.

Faster than most could follow, Clint bent sideways and his boot connected with the leaper's solar plexus.

The attacker froze in midair like a character in a cartoon. Backer heard him gasping as first the knife, then the man himself fell to earth.

On stage, the girl moaned her love song.

The other man flicked a glance at the glistening K-bar on the sand, inches away.

Backer stood just behind the abandoned knife, waiting.

Anxious and still-angry eyes went from the knife on the sand to Backer, just beyond it.

"Take your turn or find another merry-go-round," Backer yelled above the din.

The other man took in Backer, from the overhung brow to the muscles in his bare, too casually held arms.

Mumbling defiance, Backer's opponent licked his lips and walked backward until the mob swallowed him.

Clint stepped over the fallen man and moved to the stage. His brother Colt was no longer in sight.

Backer crossed his arms on the lip of the platform, next to Roper and rested his chin on his tattooed forearm. Above him, the singer gave him a smile.

"Pretty easy duty," said Clint, "huh, Rope?"

"Too easy," the other biker mumbled. "I coulda stayed a grunt in Saigon and had more jollies than this. Does Wulff think we're bikers or just two-bit mercenaries?"

"Is there a difference?"

The leaner man remained silent.

Backer shouted above the music, "Where'd Colt get to?"

Roper spit. "Baby brother is pushin' eighteen, Clint my man. You don't stop sittin' on him, he's gonna grow sideways steada straight up."

Suddenly Backer's fingers covered Roper's arm and squeezed gently. "There ain't no profit messin' in family business."

"Colt's my friend, man." Roper's blue eyes met Backer's reddish pair. "And time was, so were you, big brother Clint. You wanna step out and erase them days?"

Backer's forefinger tapped Roper's sleeve. They both heard the *thud.* "My bones against your blade?"

"You sings the song, I hums the tune," Roper said expressionlessly. "Call it, Second Rider."

There was a pause in the ocean of sound, and quick as an adder Backer's hand was gone from Roper's arm.

"Sorry, man." He ripped off his bandanna and wiped his face. "Ever since I snatched Colt from that Okie Home, I been like a mama hen. Nerves are bad. Apologies."

Roper remained motionless, as he had throughout the encounter. "All you ever had was nerve." He looked up at the stage where the girl was beginning to sing again. "You lose that, ol' Scout, and what'll you have left in your hand to bet on?"

"Maybe as nothing as you." Backer grinned. "Except for my Baby Bro."

For the first time the thin man moved, flicking a thumb toward the trailers where the offices were. "Colt went yonder, after Aubrey."

Clint frowned. "This gig was Wulff's setup. I don't dig Colt getting too close to Favereu. He smells like good old downright-upright establishment trouble."

"More trouble 'n you?" Roper called as Backer moved on.

Backer chuckled. "Guess there ain't nonesuch, is there?"

But the laughter died in his throat when he saw Colt outside the Favereu trailer arguing with a gaunt, dark man as the smaller figure of Favereu tugged impatiently at Colt's elbow.

Clint shook his head. Colt was high again. Be lucky to make it through this gig without a stay in the stone hotel, maybe even a trip back to that Oklahoma hellhole, since Colt wouldn't turn eighteen 'til April.

He was close enough now to hear the words and to see the pamphlets in the dark man's hands—and the cross around his neck.

Clint sighed. With the stuff that was shooting through him, Colt would argue with a Krishna at an airport. As if there was really a *truth* you could find the end of, like a ball of twine, if only you argued loudly with anybody crazy enough to believe anything . . .

He came up behind Colt and put his hand softly on his brother's shoulder as Favereu stepped back.

"*You* talk sense into him," Favereu snapped at Clint. "I'm paying you muscle-and-leather clowns enough."

Ignoring the promoter, Colt whirled on his older brother, a scrap of cheap yellow paper in his fist. "This dude thinks he's got it nailed," he snarled. His eyes, which had the same reddish-tint as his brother's, were cat's-eye slits. More meth. One of these days soon . . .

Clint shook off the thought as he saw the crudely lettered header: *The Only Love That Gets You Free.*

"I want him to follow me while I check the gate." Favereu's white collar was wilting, merging into the yellow paisley shirt. "I don't pay for philosophical debates between tramps."

"Favereu thinks he sneezes lightning over this world," Clint said, "just because he's pilin' up all those green pictures of presidents. Don't you, Aubrey?"

The promoter tugged at his beads. "I pay for what I get. Maybe you thugs don't realize—"

Clint stepped in front of Favereu and tapped the little cross around the stranger's neck. "And all you dudes on the other side of the lookin' glass think you got the road map. You and the druids and the witches and the Buddhists and Alice and the White Rabbit. You all got the answer. And I'll be damned if I ever knew what the question was."

"That's the question," Colt whispered to his older brother, his vocal cords drug-tight.

"I want one of you bikers to come with me," Favereu snarled, "and I want him now."

"Damnation!" Colt hissed. "Brother Love here knows how to slip out from under it! We don't even gotta be afraid of dyin' anymore, do we, little Brother Love?"

"Don't be damned." The dark man turned to Clint. "And you know—" For a moment their eyes clicked, and it was Clint who found himself breaking the contact. "—you know the question."

"Brother Love—" Colt snatched the dark man by his beard and pulled him forward. "You is just so little for so much mouth."

With an effortless movement of his head, the gaunt man slipped his beard out of Colt's clutching hand. "Only answer to death is life. And there's a lot more life for you than what you've got."

Clint's head was buzzing. The heat, the afternoon altercations, the constant screaming—how could it be worth the bread Favereu would pay them? Weren't they bikers so they could be free of the Man? But he was *Second* Rider. It was Wulff who was leader—Wulff who took the contract with Favereu.

"I ain't afraid of Mister Death, and I ain't afraid of your spooky jive, Brother Love," Colt shouted, pulling the dark man forward by his ragged shirt.

"There's more than numbness from fluid flowing through you. Joy doesn't come through a needle."

His head rocked back as Colt struck him in the face.

Swiftly Clint surveyed the dark man, deciding that he was basically unhurt despite the trickle of blood at his nose.

"Now," Favereu repeated, ignoring the violence.

Over his shoulder Clint saw that the dark man hadn't moved. No sense in these religious guys . . . No sense at all.

He raised Colt's clenched fist, uncoiled the fingers. A blue paper tube of quarters rested in the palm.

"Stupid toys. You're gonna bust your fingers some hot day."

Colt flipped the roll. "Me and President George, we do the best we can." He stuck the roll in the pocket of his jeans and looked up at Clint. "We ain't no Kung Fu King Kong like you."

"I only know what a man learns on the streets," Clint said quietly. "If you don't start to think, you ain't gonna be on the streets long enough to learn."

Colt shambled away after Favereu. "I hit that little guy hard as I could and he took it," Colt mumbled. "That makes a man think."

As his brother and the promoter disappeared into the crowd, Clint turned back toward the Favereu trailer, but found the dark man in his path. Suddenly at a loss, he blurted, "You're scrawny, but you must be tougher 'n cowhide. Colt says he gave you everything he had."

"So did Rome," said the dark man, the blood drying in his beard. Clint paused for a moment, unable to make sense of the words, then went on to the Favereu trailer.

When he looked back, neither his brother nor the dark man could be seen through the mob.

"You."

"Me."

Clint recognized Harry Blackburn, who, along with Rex Aikens and Favereu, made up the triumvirate of FaveRock Productions, responsible for the festival and for the employment of the Wolves. Blackburn stood just outside the FaveRock trailer door.

Tall and thin, wearing his tan suit with its murderously narrow lapels unrumpled, Blackburn regarded Clint Backer through owlish amber-tinted sunglasses.

"Commere." He mounted the two steps, unlocked and entered the trailer. Backer followed.

The interior was cool and dark. Blackburn stood with

his hand on the knob of an opened inner door. "Well, come on."

"Why sure." Backer entered the inner office, where an air conditioner's hum filled the room and ruffled the velvet drapes over the sliding glass door.

Blackburn sat on the edge of Favereu's big black desk. Favereu, Backer suspected, would not appreciate the familiarity. But Favereu's leather swivel chair was empty.

"Aubrey's got one of your people with him now, checking the gate," Blackburn said, his eyes invisible behind the frames.

"One of my people?" Backer frowned, slipping into the big leather chair behind the desk and swiveling to enjoy the blast of cool air.

Blackburn started to protest, checked himself, then leaned across the desk. "You *are* a motorcycle . . . uh . . . person, aren't you?"

Backer sighed, feeling droplets of perspiration cool beneath his vest. "Mostly. You *are* an Aubrey Favereu . . . uh . . . person?"

Blackburn frowned. "Save the theatrics for the pros. You're getting paid. Aubrey wants to set up night delivery and patrol, and since you're leader—"

"Wulff's leader."

The lenses stared at Backer. "I've seen you. You're in charge."

"Wulff's leader. I'm Second Rider."

Blackburn slapped at a fly that buzzed over the desk. When he removed his hand, the insect struggled feebly. Blackburn was quick, Clint noted.

"There's too much going down here for games with penny-ante pirates. If you're not the leader, then go and get him and bring him back . . . fast."

"It's hot," Backer said quietly. His thumb reached across the desk, too fast for Blackburn to follow, and gently thumped an amber lens. "Cool here."

Blackburn stared at Clint. The biker smiled.

Abruptly the promoter whirled, then swung open the door to the foyer. "Tell me where to find him then and get out. Don't think Aubrey won't hear about the kind of service his cash is buying."

A stiff pause, with only the AC hum. Then Backer was up and out the door. "I'll wait and tell him myself," he said. He was careful to bump against Blackburn as he passed. His hunch was right: the man was carrying iron. What level of power had Wulff tied them into? And why did the big boys need two hundred motorcycle bandits to keep a pack of crazy hippies in line?

He flopped onto a couch in the antechamber. "Sometimes a man's got to lower his expectations."

Blackburn slammed the inner door behind him. "Where's your leader?"

Backer flipped up his thick left wrist, around which a Rolex was incongruously wrapped, souvenir of a Reno poker game. "He's a dude that looks like Lon Chaney, Jr." He yawned. "S'posed to be at the vans about now, for check-in with the Scout."

"Who's the Scout?"

Backer grinned. "I am." *And I might as well be punching a time clock*, he thought.

"Then why aren't you there?"

"Because I'm here, Harry."

Blackburn hesitated, checked the lock to the inner office, jerked open the outer door. Heat and noise howled in.

"Stay here then. When I bring your leader back to

meet Aubrey, don't think they won't hear about this." The
door slammed against the blast.

"But I do," Backer said to the empty room. "Think,
that is. But it only messes your head up, Harry."

"What?"

A stout man with a western shirt, a string tie, and
three chins stood on the outside steps.

Embarrassed at having been caught talking to himself, Backer assumed an elaborately relaxed pose—arms
behind head, boots swung up onto a coffee table where
they nudged against a portable cassette player and a stack
of cassettes scattered over a copy of *Rolling Stone*. "I say,
nice day . . . if it don't rain."

"Where's Harry?"

Backer flapped a hand. "Bye bye Blackburn."

The chins trembled. "What? . . . Who are you?"

Backer sighed. Whatever games FaveRock was playing,
Rex Aikens had obviously bought in with cash, not brains.

"Harry had an errand. He left me in charge," Backer
enunciated carefully, "so's nobody swipes the trailer."

"But I have to tell him . . . Who *are* you?"

Still speaking carefully, Clint said, "Me Backer."

"You're . . . a biker?"

"Mostly. But me always a Backer."

Rex had sailed into the foyer like a deflating balloon.
He jiggled the handle of the inner office, found it locked,
and satisfied himself that neither Blackburn nor Favereu
was present.

"I hafta . . . hafta get a message to Aubrey."

"Leave it with me."

Rex almost giggled. He snatched the cassette player
from beneath Backer's heels, pulled out a key, and
unlocked the door to the inner office.

"Go away now."

Backer shook his head. The staring contest was very brief. Aikens pulled shut the inner door, locked it carefully, and moved to the far end of the office before speaking quietly into the tape player, lips to inset mike.

Outside the door, Backer got up and stretched. He really *should* be back at the vans. Wulff liked to keep his claws carefully on the gang's pulse. And Backer was Second Rider—the Scout.

But in a defiant gesture he reclosed the outer door and stepped back into the foyer. From the inner office, Aikens's voice dribbled faintly.

"Wolves."

The word was unmistakable. Backer was very still for a moment, then padded softly to the inner door.

A moment later Aikens finished his taped message, left a scrawled note on the desk, and emerged from the inner office.

Before he closed the door behind him, rattling the latch to determine that it had locked, Backer had dived for the couch and was leafing through the *Stone* magazine.

"You really should go." Aikens frowned.

"I promised." Backer flipped a page.

The fat man tested the inner door again, sighed, and opened the outer door. "Don't do anything," he said.

Backer shook his head, and as soon as Aikens's tread was off the steps, he was down on his knees, rummaging through the clutter of the coffee table. A clear plastic ruler lay on some sales charts. He slipped it against the sloped outer dowel of the door latch, worked it back and forth a little, and suddenly the door swung wide; there was the black desk, the note, and the cassette player.

"Just like in the movies." Backer breathed again as he

popped out the cartridge, crumpled the note, relocked the office, and was gone from the trailer.

———

He approached the Wolves' designated parking area. Music still blasted all about him, and the heat refused to die as he came to the hundred and ninety-six gleaming Harley Davidsons and Triumphs and the six black-and-silver vans, each with the snarling wolf's-head logo painted on their sides.

He cracked open the rear doors of the nearest van, flipped the lid of an ice chest, and drew out a Lone Star beer. Then he climbed forward, turned on the ignition, hit the temperature control, and slipped Aikens's cassette into the deck.

A few minutes later, chuckling, he drew a crumpled Marlboro from his vest and lit it. "Aaaa—maaazing." He exhaled as the tape rewound.

The last of Aikens's words—*bust insurance*—still hung in the cab, along with the blue Marlboro smoke, when the cigarette was suddenly ripped from Backer's lips, taking skin with it.

He cursed. Behind him Shannon, white-blonde ironed hair brushing her shoulders, huddled at the back of the van, cupping the cigarette.

"Shannon, honey, you're Wulff's chick. Wulff's the leader."

"Cigarettes and loyalty to leaders can be hazardous to your health and all that jive." She inched back against the cooler. "Ask the riders who came back on platters from the Nam."

"Shannon," he said quietly, not moving, "don't."

Her wide gray eyes were clouded as she cracked open the rear door and threw out the smoke. "You don't act like you're scared of the monster number Wulff pulls on people's heads."

Backer sighed. "Not scared . . . Me or Colt. Should be, probably. Just too stupid."

"You Backer brothers," Shannon snorted, "are not stupid . . . Just crazy. You don't act like you're afraid of nothin'."

He answered vacantly, gazing out the tinted windshield. "Maybe that's just what I'm afraid of . . . Nothin'."

Shannon laughed. "And that younger brother of yours—he wouldn't cluck if you stuck an ice pick in his ear. You brought him to the pack too young, Clint."

"Where else did I have to go?" He squinted. "And I give you eight to five he's no more 'n a year behind you, lady."

"Nobody," she answered, eyes clouding, "is as old as me."

"And Wulff's still my friend." His head rested against the seat as he realized how the definition of that word had changed through the years. "Kind of . . . Sort of."

"I thought you liked to fight. You could take him. I bet you could. You could be First Rider."

He turned down the air, lowered the window, and looked at her. "Sweetheart, I don't wanna *be* First Rider."

She stared. "Never figured you for gutless, Clint."

Again he sighed. "I never figured me for anything. I'm just a square hare in a round rabbit hole. I'm a biker 'cause the entry fee's low and the dress code ain't high."

"C'mon." She sounded nervous. "So Wulff's your friend and he's mean. Forget it."

His reddish eyes stared through the bug-flecked windshield. "If I wasn't a biker, guess I'd be one of those hippies, in beads and body paint—"

"I've seen you move, Clint. You could never wimp out."

"Ten years ago I'da been a beat." He laughed, and the sound made Shannon shiver. "Just one of those airheads lookin' for the biggest outfit to be a misfit in. Maybe Colt's right. Maybe someplace things make sense."

"Wulff seems to like things fine." She sounded surly.

Backer nodded without turning. "Me 'n Wulff seen a lotta bad road. There's some guys that like holding other people's lives in their hands, and some of 'em like busting 'em up. I just leave 'em be and get along as best I can, minding business."

She squirmed up behind his chair. "You make Wulff sound—"

"I'm purely evil, sweetness."

They both jumped.

Wulff had his large head stuck through the cab window, resting on crossed wrists.

Backer saw how the last of the sunlight outlined each hair on the white skin of his arms, and he wondered again why Wulff never tanned.

"Didn't hear your machine, and I didn't hear your boots." Backer stared into his eyes. "You levitate, Mister Wizard?"

Wulff returned the stare, his coarse black beard stretched in a grin.

"Just flew in from Oz." He jerked his head back toward the camp. "Ol' Aubrey seems to want a lot for his coin."

"Not just Aubrey. Blackburn should be over here anytime looking for you."

Wulff nodded. "I was easy to find. Says one of my men gave him lip. You Backers got more lip 'n anybody but Mick Jagger. Was it you gave Blackburn the chill?"

Clint leaned back. "Honest work gives me labor pains."

Before Wulff could respond, Backer had the cassette from Favereu's office spinning. "But then this ain't exactly honest work, is it?"

They sat in silence, Wulff resting against the window frame, Backer with his boots on the dash, Shannon leaning over the seat as Aikens's tape played through.

Colt joined them in time for the climax.

The others were silent. Colt was genuinely amused. "How could they be so stupid?" He laughed. "All that dope for bust insurance and a—a blimp like Aikens tips their hand."

Clint shrugged. "A gig this size is bound to get looked at close. Not bad thinking to have a scapegoat close to hand. They just made a mistake using a bozo like Aikens as a pawn." He paused. "The Wolves aren't pawns . . . are we, Wulff?"

In answer, Wulff held up a tire iron in one hefty paw. "The tape said Aikens stashed the stuff in one of the caps. Time for hide and seek, boys and girls."

It was in the left rear hubcap of the second van they tried. Colt popped it off, saw the plastic bags of white powder fall loose, and whooped, "It's here! Just like findin' the prize in the Crackerjacks!"

Triumphantly he held up a glove, and by the sun's dying rays they all saw the plastic bags full of white powder.

"They pay high premiums for their insurance," Clint remarked, tasting the dust.

"Easy to find, and fine stuff, no doubt, if anyone comes lookin'." Wulff ran a hand through his thick black hair. "Now all we gotta do is figure out a proper payback for ol' Aubrey."

"Let's kill 'em and eat 'em," Colt said cheerfully, peering over his brother's shoulder.

"No." Clint glanced up at the setting sun. "The biggest set of the day is due to start at 11." He glanced at his brother. "Can you fetch Godzilla and keep your mouth shut to everybody else?"

Colt scratched his chin. "Two things at one and the very same time. Golly whiz, I can try, Captain Blood."

Wulff nodded. "Shannon, get the chicks, spread the word. Have everybody ready to ride out at 11."

She was gone.

"Clever, clever Scout," Wulff said when they were alone. "You think of checking this inspiration out with me? Or was there a *coup d'etat* while I was stoned?"

"Sorry, man." Clint crouched forward. "But I think you'll dig it, and it'll blast the Nehru jacket clean offa Aubrey's back. Listen . . ."

———

The big English group was late starting. They began their set by floodlight; everything beyond the stage was Texas-country evening black.

Far away, inside the cool inner office, Aubrey Favereu leaned back in his chair, fingertips pressed together, listening to Blackburn reel off a list of figures. He nodded approvingly.

Aikens, at the far end of the table, coughed nervously.

Aubrey glanced at him. "An objection, Rex?"

Rex shook his wide head. "It's good profit," he said. There was a pile of currency, carefully counted and recounted, before him. "But we're just middle-level guys, Aubrey. And the big boys are giving us some bad stuff for the amount of profit involved. I got half a dozen dealers complaining. If the lid rips—"

"It won't," Favereu snapped.

"But if does—" Rex persisted.

Blackburn, still wearing the amber shades, glanced up from his own pile of cash and stared at the fat promoter.

"Then we have the bikers to blame. And we can prove it with what you planted on them."

Aikens was really sweating. "I know that stuff is bad, that's why the profit margin's so high. But we may have to throw the Wolves to the wolves," he giggled, "if you get my meaning. Like I said on that tape memo this afternoon—"

Aubrey's hand slapped the desk, and a few bills floated upward. "What memo? Aikens, you—"

As the British band sang, as the crowd cheered, as the promoters sat around their table, the Wolves were working.

Most of the pack was in the parking area, in formation, engines humming, unheard under the blast of sound.

Godzilla, the three-hundred-pound sergeant-at-arms, reached casually up the side of a stake and pulled a monolithic speaker off its perch. Torn wires crackled in the darkness. No one seemed to notice or care. Other speakers joined the paraphernalia piled outside the FaveRock trailer, just beyond the drape-covered glass. Under quiet, eager hands a makeshift ten-foot ramp emerged—one end on the ground, the other upraised to the middle of the glass door.

Backer wheeled his Harley to the edge of the ramp. He could hear Colt, astride his golden Triumph, behind him. Godzilla stood patiently to one side. Wulff and Roper kicked their machines alive.

Inside, Rex had finished his story of the memo, and the inner room had been searched for the cassette. Blackburn was about to open the outer door when Clint whispered, "Wagooonnns ho!" and roared forward over the plank, shutting his eyes briefly as the glass shattered. Then his machine was thundering, circling inside the small confines of the office like a dinosaur in a kennel.

Harry leaned against the overturned desk and slipped a hand inside his jacket. It came out with a .38.

With a *twanggg* Roper's blade transfixed Blackburn's tan sleeve to the table edge as the riders circled the hedged-in promoters.

"I can use this," Rex said shakily, pointing the short barrel of a .22 into Roper's ear.

"Wrong." Clint threw him aside and took the gun, all in one motion.

"I owe you." Roper retrieved his blade.

"Put it on your tab." Clint jerked down Blackburn's jacket.

"You can't . . . They'll hear you—" Aubrey spluttered as his shirt was jerked roughly down, pinioning his arms.

But the band played, and the crowd cheered, and the FaveRock trailer was far from view.

In their psychedelic underwear, the promoters were bound to their chairs. Favereu began trying to work loose his gag.

"Well, lookahere," Colt said, off his bike and scrabbling at a floorboard.

"You find the hidey-hole?" Wulff asked, gliding forward.

Colt reached in and began extracting bags of powder, tablets, and cash.

"That'll pay for one fine, easy summer," Wulff observed quietly.

Aubrey had worked loose his gag. "You don't know who you're dealing with, you punk outlaws. You've bit more hassle than you can swallow."

Lazily Wulff waved a bag of powder under the furious promoter's nose. "You been playin' outa your league, Aubrey, my man. Your people will go for you, not us. We got this . . ." In his other glove he held the cassette. "And if you're playin' with the pros, they'll know we'll have this"—he held up the powder—"ingested or dealt before they're done expressin' their displeasure with you. It's a write-off for 'em." He patted the promoter's cheek. "And so are you."

Favereu was still screaming as they roared out the jagged glass hole. But Clint had watched Colt quietly pick up a plastic bag and thrust it into his leathers. Clint said nothing, but Colt suddenly cried out, "Looka this! I musta kept it this afternoon, and ol' Aubrey got it mixed in with his stash!" He laughed, tossing the cheap yellow pamphlet with its crudely drawn cross into the air.

Their machines jumped out of the trailer, took their place in the dark at the head of the waiting pack, and howled through the camp, trailed by Aubrey's screams and the band's music.

At the gate Wulff, at the head of the pack, slowed. The dark, gaunt man was outlined in his headlight, and Wulff would have to either swerve or run him down.

The man didn't move, and Clint, Second Rider, saw the light reflect off the stranger's eyes.

Wulff suddenly twisted his throttle, banked sharply to the left, and curved by the gaunt man. Clint followed, avoiding the dark man's stare.

The other bikes and vans followed their leaders, and two hundred machines twisted past the unmoving man and then were ripping through the Texas night.

THE RANCH

*T*he Wolves howled across Texas in the smoke of wildly spent cash the fire of heated debates about their next destination.

Over I-45, weaving through Houston traffic, butterfly carburetors opened wide, they lunged onto I-10 and roared west, racing the night.

Through Sealy and Columbus, past Flatonia and Schuser, into mellow San Antonio and out the other side, racing the rising sun, they sliced through the dust that covered the five hundred and sixty-three miles between the festival and El Paso.

Shannon stirred within her parka, behind Wulff.

"Where we goin' this time, Wulff?"

Wulff raised a dusty black glove and pointed into the wind.

"Sure . . . but where in particular?"

She felt the big man's shrug.

"Someplace else."

At a 76 truck stop near the border, the riders dismounted stiffly. Customers in the all-night diner quieted as the pack tumbled in.

"Where you guys headed?" The waitress with the beehive hairdo brought out the first shipment of steak and eggs.

Colt bit into his bleeding steak. "Someplace else."

Clint, the pack's Scout, spread a battered map across a countertop and jabbed a dusty forefinger at a tiny speck.

"Red River." His rust-colored eyes glittered across the table at Wulff. "Just like in the flicks. Little hinky Duke Wayne-type mountain town. Word is, there's gonna be a run up there next week. I'll bet the locals don't know it. Bikes from all over the U.S. of A. They'll chew up the place so good, there won't be bones left to swallow."

Wulff grinned, showing his tiny white teeth beneath the black beard. "Not if we get there first."

But when the caravan halted at midday, while cutting across the panhandle, Colt's absence was discovered.

"I know where he's gone," Clint said grimly. "You travel. We'll catch up before you're halfway to Red River."

"You're always runnin' off," Wulff grumbled.

"And they're always catchin' up," said Roper smiling.

"G'wan, run and hide. You crazy Backer brothers." Wulff showed his teeth again.

"Maybe someday we'll use up all the places there are to run." Backer's Harley disappeared in a swirl of yellow dust.

He found Colt's Triumph just where he expected. It was leaning on its kickstand before a ramshackle ranch building halfway to Woodward in the Oklahoma panhandle.

Backer sat his bike on the rise above, wrists crossed over his handlebars.

"Colter, why," he asked, "can't you let history be history?" He drove down the hill.

At the sound of the engine, Colt stepped onto the wooden porch. He was wearing what Clint thought of as his look: wide eyes, pale skin beneath the windburn, vein in the temple throbbing.

Swearing silently, Backer dismounted, climbed the wooden stairs, and greeted the deeply-tanned woman with the slash of cheekbones who had followed Colt out the screen door.

"Hello, Ma."

Colt slapped him on the shoulder. "Knew you'd show up." He opened the screen. "Ma was just reminiscing about you. C'mon in and sit a spell. Ma'd probably like to bake us an apple pie." He chuckled. "Just what you were sayin', huh, Ma?"

Without looking back, the woman reached behind her and slammed the screen in her younger boy's face. "You want food, you work for it," she said. "There's cows need milkin'."

"And what's Harvey doin'?" Colt asked. "Out huntin'?" His voice quavered, and Clint was embarrassed for him. "He can kill a fifth of Old Crow faster than anybody in these parts."

"Your stepfather is ailin'." She turned her back and went inside. The brothers followed.

"Then we'll pay for it, fond mother." Colt stood on the circular rug in the little living room and tugged wadded-up bills from his jeans. "Here . . . A hundred bucks for a piece of pie." He dropped the money on top of the old Zenith television set.

A sweep of her hand sent the money fluttering to the floor. "It's dirty . . . I know it. *You're* dirty. You always were."

Kneeling, Colt scooped up the cash and carefully replaced it on the Zenith, next to the antenna. His fingers trembled as he laid out more bills.

She ignored the money. "Are the police after you?"

"No, Ma. Look . . . There's two hundred . . . Three . . . Five . . . Five hundred bucks for a piece of pie."

"Colt . . ." Backer put his hand on his brother's shoulder. "Let's go."

Suddenly the old woman screamed, "Yes, take him! You did it before!"

Through clenched teeth Backer said, "I took him when you threw him away."

"We sent him to that Home for his own good! There was a chance for him! He was my baby, my good baby. It was you, Clinton, never was no good."

"No," Clint said, "I guess I never was."

"Your real dad tried to beat the fear of the Lord into you, but I looked at those eyes of yours and knew it was useless. When you took off on that sickle, I praised God!"

"Amen." Opening the door Backer said, "Let's ride, Colt."

With surprising speed the old woman raced ahead of them, yanking the screen shut. "Why did you have to drag Colter into damnation? Why?"

Backer leaned against the door frame, an arm around his brother's thin shoulders. "Ma, you 'n Harvey told the social worker Colt was 'incorrigible.' I know. How many times did you visit that place they put him? How many?"

She looked away, her face drawn so tight it was little more than skin over skull. "When they'd turned him back into my baby boy again, we would've fetched him."

Flinging off his brother's arm Colt cried, "It was Clint, Ma, Clint that came barrelin' up to that place on his hog. We were having calisthenics. At least that's what they called it. Mr. Walsh had me doin' fifty extra push-ups for not payin' attention.

"'I'll take care of you, kid.' That's all Clint said. I hopped on and never once looked back. Clint took me to the pack, where they accept me just like I am. And they ain't afraid. Not of the Man. Not of dyin'. Not of nothin'."

There was scorn in her laugh. "Fool. Scum like that accept you just so long as you swagger like a cheap tough. Wait 'til they find out how scared you really are, boy. Your ma knows."

"I'm not afraid anymore . . . of anything. Clint taught me."

"My little baby Colter, who had the nightmares even at naptime!" She was screaming. "You belong back in that Home!"

"Ma, I'm a man grown, or nearly."

A slurred voice came from the bedroom. "Lucille, what's all that racket?"

"Just some kids goin' by on sickles. Go back to sleep." She pushed Colt hard in the chest. He stumbled against his brother. "Go on, take him! Take my baby back to Hell!"

As they rode away, the two bikes traveling abreast, Backer called over, "I'll take care of you, kid."

His brother laughed. "You heard the lady." His Triumph shot forward. "Let's go to Hell!"

———

The next morning the Backers rejoined the gang north of Albuquerque, the sun an orange ball of flame over the gas stations and refineries. They roared swiftly down the long hill below Santa Fe, and then it and Camel Rock too were behind them as they rolled through Taos and climbed the last crooked miles into the little mountain town that waited for them in the crisp pine-air at the end of the trail.

No one but Clint and Godzilla noticed the prim little sign planted out before the first buildings:

Red River, Colo.
Pop. 3,600.
Spend Some Time With Us.

Clint smiled tightly at the naive welcome, a tiny scar pulling at the left corner of his lip. Godzilla was late joining the gang in town. He had stopped to splinter the sign off its flimsy post and strap it to his hog for a souvenir.

"Postcards gets lost," he said

THE TOWN

It had been a shank-bruising, bone-rattling, all-night ride, but the Wolves rolled into the unsuspecting mountain town a day before the scheduled run.

Colt, pulse pounding with amphetamines, slammed around the road's last bend and bounced into town, the first rock of a rubber-and-chrome avalanche. His golden Triumph leaped up a pile of sagging boardwalk steps, and an impossibly hard left sent him rocketing past the just-opened shops, the wood-thump and machine-growl making heads pop against windows and out of doors.

An elderly woman with a pink complexion poked her head out of a tea shop doorway.

As the Triumph swept past her, she shouted over her shoulder, "Annie, call the State Troopers!"

She flinched at the Triumph's sudden squeal of brakes.

Delicately, Colt rolled the golden machine back to the tea shop entrance.

"Morning, ladies."

"A fine morning you'll have when the Troopers arrive!"

Colt leaned over his handlebars, a hundred dollar bill between his fingers. "Fine day to be alive . . . if you recall the sensation." He flicked the bill into the shop doorway.

It was snatched away. "Let's mind our business, Annie." The door slammed, and the *Sorry, We Are Closed* sign was slapped against the glass.

"A fine day to be alive," Colt repeated, his bike stuttering down the porch steps.

Then, after a pause, "Anyway, it's a fine day."

The Wolves were a new shock wave for the little town, but by no means the first assault it had endured since its inception in the days when miners had grabbed the land in both fists and ripped the precious metals from the earth's depths. The gold and silver and the great mining companies were gone now; the only reminder of the wealth ripped away were the chunks of granite-sprayed silver or gold in tourist shop windows.

Nor, ironically, was the town unfamiliar with wild men loaded down with whiskey and revolvers who fought and even, according to town legend, died, too slow on the draw, their blood seeping into the dust of Main Street.

Postcards were available with the consumptive likeness of Doc Halliday, who passed through on his last journey to a resort in Glenwood Springs.

There were pen-and-ink sketches of Wyatt Earp and Bat Masterson too, though their likenesses owed more to the recent television serials, and their destiny was less dramatic. Masterson died a sedate sportswriter in Denver, and Earp disappeared in a cloud of scandal. But dangerous men they were to know, and old-timers spoke proudly of their grandfathers achieving a first-name familiarity with ancient desperadoes.

Now the savagery had come again, with the howl of

the Wolves as they roared and screamed and tore their way
into the streets, and the town paused with its collective
finger on the telephone dial and sniffed the scent of freely
spent cash that was carried along on the mountain breeze.

The Wolves hungrily sunk their fangs into the meat of
Red River as the pack spilled through the dusty streets,
vacation crowds, and Saturday commotion.

Wulff swerved inches past a lumbering pickup-
camper. Hearing the driver curse, Shannon looked over her
shoulder and stuck out her tongue. In the camper, the
teenage rider beside the driver smiled back at her.

Colt veered to avoid a frantically confused yellow dog
and found his Triumph again stuttering up boardwalk
steps. He pulled back desperately as the pharmacy door
went down beneath his wheels. He whined to a stop, his
front tire brushing the counter.

An older man with yellowish skin and spectacles
brushed splinters from his smock and pushed the greasy
stub of a pencil over an invoice pad. "Estimate damage at
eighty dollars and change. Or I can call the Troopers."

Colt threw down another hundred. "Iodine too,
OK?"

A red-haired waitress slouched in her doorway,
watching the yellow dog scramble away. She flicked hair
from her eyes and coughed.

"Lousy dust. Lousy town. Lousy bikers."

Clint noticed the sign above her, its unlit neon spelling
out DARBY'S BAR & DANCE. It hung lopsidedly, as if
dropped by a negligent giant. His gaze traveled downward
to the waitress, and he shut off his Harley.

"Ain't we got dust enough without you hooligans
horsin' around?" she asked, a towel dangling from her
apron.

"You know better 'n me." He jerked the kickstand and climbed the steps. Where the Scout's bike was seen, the rest of the pack would follow.

"You like dust, I guess?" She eyed him as he entered.

"Nope. But horsin' around's okay."

Other riders shouldered in.

"Shoot all," the waitress observed. "Who're you—Wild Bill Hickok?"

"Nope." He patted her cheek and moved on to a table. "I'm thirsty."

The room filled with the odors of leather and grease as an ancient jukebox cleared its throat and belched out the sound of the Jefferson Airplane.

Spyder, the one-handed rider, had his hook sunk into the back of the machine, sending the volume up to the maximum. The windows shook.

"How about some slosh, Rope?" Clint called, leaning back.

Roper vaulted the bar, and a full pitcher sailed across the room. "Heads up!"

Backer caught the jug and a face full of foam.

"Good doggy, Roper."

"Woof and woof." Roper poured a frosty pitcher over his own head, gasping as the cool liquid hit fevered flesh.

A little man with an angry onion-face and a red flannel shirt burst from the back room.

"Just what is this?"

"This is Darby's Bar & Dance," Roper explained, "such as it is."

"Just egg-zactly what it is. I run it, and you bums can't—"

"Is you Darby?" Godzilla, the three-hundred-pound sergeant-at-arms, inquired gently.

The angry onion-face bobbed up and down over the flannel collar. "You bums can't just swagger in here and—"

"S' nice place, Droopy," Godzilla said. "Ain't been washed since Noah parked the ark, no offense."

Wulff filled the doorway, flopped down next to Clint, and poured foaming fluid from the pitcher down his white throat.

In the street there was a screech, and through the dirty window they saw Colt's Triumph do an almost perfect three hundred and sixty to avoid a pickup.

"He'll bust that Triumph's guts one day soon," Clint muttered.

"He'll bust his neck long before then." Wulff wiped his mouth with the back of a paw.

Snatching the half-empty pitcher from Wulff's surprised fingers, Darby screeched, "The cops will bust all your guts before you got the time to swallow."

"Ahh . . ." Wulff grinned. "Mine host." He turned to Clint. "Please to oil the squeak, Backer."

From his leathers Clint withdrew a plump beaded pouch. Carefully he withdrew three one hundred dollar bills.

"Keep a little something for yourself, my man."

The little man stared down at the bills in his hand.

"He knows what it is, you s'pose?" Wulff wondered.

"Money, it is," Godzilla yelled into Darby's ear. "Y' know, it pays for things that get used up and busted." Then he added apologetically, "A lot of stuff around us gets used up and busted."

"And will it cover damage to the Backer brothers when we get used up and busted?" Clint wondered, hearing Colt's Triumph whine through the streets.

Wulff cocked a pointed brow. "Whadidyasay?"

Backer shook off the thought. *Morbid . . . Getting too old for cowboys and clodhopper games.*

Darby crinkled a bill, rubbed its sides together.

"S' real," Wulff told him. "Gen-u-wine Yankee cash. And there won't be no theft reports on it. Check it out."

Darby spluttered, "This ain't gonna last, the way you bums are—"

"Do let us know when you need more for your Christmas sockey-wockey," Backer said, wiping foam from his lips.

"I needs a refill, Dopey." Wulff held out the pitcher.

The proprietor eyed the paper in one hand and the empty pitcher in the other. His little pink tongue traced a circle around his mouth as he stared.

"Fetch," Backer said quietly.

Darby looked up. "What . . . uh, what's your brand?"

"Just whatever the house has for sale," Wulff told him. "The Wolves are tickled to death with whatever's for sale."

"Is there anything not for sale?" Backer wondered, watching the proprietor waddle off, mumbling and counting the bills as the red-haired waitress scurried from table to table.

"Good man, Dorky," Wulff remarked. "A knight in shining flannel."

"Musta been a buncha fun when he was still alive," Backer snorted.

"Y' know," Wulff leaned across the table, "this is kind of a—whaddya call it—a laboratory experiment. For once we got all the cash and party supplies we need." He glanced across the bar at Darby, busy at the tap. "We can push this town right to the edge."

"Why?" asked Backer.

Wulff let loose his patented throat-deep chuckle. "To see. It's perfect. Ol' Aubrey won't dare report the loss of his ill-gotten gains, and we can bend this town 'til its spine snaps and then say, 'Put it on the tab.'"

"What's the fun in that?"

"Because we'll see," Wulff whispered, "we'll just see. Everything's for sale. Everything."

Briefly Backer wondered sadly if the leader was right. But Wulff interrupted himself.

"Quail yonder," he commented. Backer saw a group of college girls, obvious non-locals, clustered about a table. He rose and moved to them.

"Mind if I set a spell?" he asked politely, towering over the table.

"Would it mean just a whole lot if we said no?" a blonde answered. Another girl giggled.

Backer nodded. "For certain sure. I'd hafta . . . go someplace else."

"So go someplace else," the first girl said, and the group laughed.

"Let it be." He gripped the table's edge and dragged it ten feet across the floor. He then hoisted the blonde off the floor, still in her chair, and plunked her down at the rim.

"Now we're someplace else."

The blonde spluttered but stayed. Others joined them.

"So what do you do?" the blonde asked him a little later as the red-haired waitress scurried through the din and Darby kept scribbling up the spiraling tab.

"Do? We survive." Clint drank.

"You don't make it sound very exciting."

He shrugged. "We're free."

"But don't you have . . . anyone important . . . anyone special?"

"There are no important people." Clint smiled.

"No . . . important people," the blonde repeated, then abruptly drained her glass.

Another screech came from the street. The group in the bar glanced out the window in time to see Colt's Triumph skid sideways, bounce off a curb, and topple over on him. The engine died.

Colt let the Triumph's warm yellow metal rest against him. The cocaine still warmed him, and he didn't mind the pressure.

Then his face narrowed. Beyond his handlebars he saw the shape of a revolver, long and black against red felt, in the gun shop window.

He pushed the bike away and walked toward the shop.

The gun waited for him. Carefully he mounted the boardwalk steps and put his hands against the glass, moving in front of the gun.

Inside, the jangling bell brought the old man to the front counter.

"Help you?" he asked nervously.

"The gun."

"Huh? Oh, you mean that there .45. That's somethin', ain't it? Over eighty years old if she's a day."

"I can see."

"Think you know guns, huh, Young Blood?" He leaned forward. "Well, lissen here, I got that from a fella twenny years ago. Got a paper says it belonged to Buffalo Bill Cody." He chuckled. "They don't got it all, them stuck-up fellas at the museum on Lookout Mountain."

Colt Backer's fingers traced the shop side of the display case.

"Not fer sale, 'course," the old man said. "Have that 'til the day I die."

Colt stared down.

"Somethin' else you need?" Then, after a silence, "You want somethin', Young Blood?"

The old man gave up, turned to straighten a box of cartridges.

When he turned back, there was a hundred dollar bill on the counter.

"Hey, mister! That there's—"

Blood-red eyes on the gun, Colt plucked bills from his jeans and dropped them in clusters on the counter.

"Fella, you got five, six hunnerd there—"

"So black," Colt whispered, still dropping cash from his fingers. "Like . . . a cobra."

"Mister, that there gun ain't fer—"

"Yeah, ol' King Cobra."

"You got eight, nine, close to a thousand dollars here! Ain't no gun worth that."

"Then it's mine." His fingers thrust right through the glass case, splinters and blood droplets splattering the floor. Carefully Colt picked up the revolver, then cradled it against his chest with his uncut hand.

"Gimme shells."

"That thing ain't been fired in years. You'll blow your fool head off."

More cash on the counter. "Right there . . . I see 'em."

The old man looked at the cash.

"I'll fix it," Colt said. "It'll work, just like when it was alive."

"Fella . . . Oh—" With a curse the man thrust a box of shells at Colt and scraped up the cash. "It ain't *my* head."

"Cody's gun," Colt whispered, thrusting it into his jacket and walking into the sunlight toward the place where his Triumph still lay sprawled in the street.

Spyder, Deacon, Porky, and three other bikers stood around the fallen bike, pulling at a young girl in a fast-food uniform.

She struggled free, bumped into Colt.

"Please . . . I have to get to work."

"Let 'er go, Colt. We seen her first," Spyder called.

"Looks like she don't wanna play," Colt responded, holding the girl.

"S' okay," Deacon answered. "We're Wolves. We pay for what we chew up . . . Remember?"

Colt still held the girl.

"I ain't heard nobody in this town complain yet," Spyder said, digging in his leathers and throwing a wad of cash toward the girl. "You ever seen that much, Hamburger Pattie?"

The money fell at her feet. "You can't buy me," she snapped, then looked up at Colt. "I'm due at work . . . please?"

The six other riders surrounded them in a semicircle.

"Sweet thing," Colt sighed, "you got the casting all wrong. You want service, call a pizza shop . . . they deliver. I ain't the Lone Ranger, I'm just the comic relief."

"We'll take her off your hands," Deacon said, reaching.

Colt pulled the woman back to him. "Then again, it ain't polite to grab."

"Thinks he's safe 'cause he's Second Rider's brother," Spyder said.

Colt laughed. "There ain't *nobody* safe in this life—is there, Spyder?"

The riders moved in close. "Little Colt thinks he's mean too."

"I ain't mean," Colt replied, looking across the semicircle.

"He admits it." Spyder grinned.

"Just crazy." The old revolver's barrel was suddenly pushed under Spyder's jaw.

"They do say the sight's last to go," Colt murmured. "Look up real quick, you'll be able to see your brains hit the boardwalk roof."

The others weren't so sure. "Bet that hunk of black iron ain't even loaded," Deacon said. "Let's take him."

"Stop, man!" Spyder cried.

"Sorry," Colt murmured in the terrified girl's ear, "the real Lone Ranger wouldn't've been caught with his mask down and without a silver bullet in the chamber." He smiled as the riders pressed in. "If they call my bluff," he whispered, shoving the barrel deeper into Spyder's throat, "you'll still have about a ten-second head start. Use it wisely." He smiled and spoke to the others. "So . . . call my hand . . . if you got the cards." He cocked the black hammer.

"Guys, hold up!" Spyder gasped, but the others disregarded him.

"Kind of interesting," Porky muttered. "Either Spyder goes out or Colt does. Even money, I say. Let's go for it."

From the cafe across the way Wulff glanced over his shoulder and commented to Clint, "Time for your eye test. Read the figures across the road from left to right."

Backer darted a bored look through the dirty window.

"Six punks who think they're tough, Colt, and . . ."

He was up, Wulff following.

At the street, Wulff caught his arm. "To the alley, where they not gonna see us comin'. Let us pedestrians pedest."

They came through the alley and mounted the board-walk. From out of nowhere Roper joined them.

"Colt and his silly toys." Roper shook his head. "Guns never go 'boom' when you want 'em too. But a blade now—"

Roper's switchblade hissed open. "How you boys fixed for blades?" he calmly asked the standoff partici-pants.

"Maybe you been leader too long, Wulff," Porky said, responding to the look in the leader's eyes.

"The floor is open for nominations," Wulff said, tak-ing a side-stance.

The possibility of blood quivered in the dusty moun-tain air. Clint knew they couldn't win, Wulff's stature as leader not withstanding. Colt was too stoned to be much use, and excluding him, six to three odds wasn't a margin to live on. But he shrugged his shoulders under the leather and stepped in front of Colt, covering him a little. When things went down, odds were Colt would be at the bottom of the pile. He might come out alive from there.

A stout old man in corduroy was suddenly in their midst.

No one had heard his approach, but there he most certainly was, half on the steps and half on the ground, effectively blocking the opposing bikers.

His one good eye glimmered under the shade of his floppy hat brim. Standing on the boardwalk in front of Colt and the girl, he said, "This is not a battlefield." His dentures clacked as he took the girl from Colt's arms.

"Where in hell did he come from?" Wulff growled.

"Not from Hell, you white-faced gargoyle." The one good eye glittered. He took an ancient black Book from under his arm and, seemingly unaware of the riders, began to flip the pages.

"Crazy old dude's some kinda priest," Deacon mumbled.

Colt eased the black revolver away from Spyder's throat.

Gratefully the rider stumbled among his companions.

"I'm a man of God, and you'll show respect," said Old One Eye.

"I'll show you my hook in your one good eye," Spyder snarled.

Clint's arm knocked him into the dirt, the hook ripping trenches through his leather sleeve.

"I am commanded to preach the Word to the heathen," the old man proclaimed, "and you boys are the heathenest I've seen for a spell."

Deacon laughed.

He ignored him. "Hush up and listen now." He began to declaim loudly from the Book, hook nose bent over the page, sun glinting off his artificial eye.

"'*Come back to me, disloyal children—it is Jehovah who speaks—*'" The old man licked his lips, skipped a bit. "'*I will take one or two from a town.*'"

"Too weird, this trip." Wulff backed away. "Somebody musta slipped acid in the beer. This is not happening."

The old man went on, hoarse now, as he attempted to shout over the roar of starting cycles. "'*To bind up hearts that are broken—*'"

Spyder swore as he rode away, but his words were covered by the engine whine.

"Just another bummer trip," Deacon growled. "One too many mushrooms in the stew." He straddled his hog. "Nobody shines like that. Nobody *talks* like that." He revved his engine, following the others. "Somebody's doin' a number on our heads."

Roper too had drifted away, as silently as he had come—smoke on the wind.

Now only the two Backers and the girl stood in front of the old man.

Clint slapped the revolver bulge that was back inside his brother's jacket. "G'wan, Stoned Ranger, before you get scared into doin' something *real* stupid."

"I ain't afraid!" Colt said. He picked up his Triumph, kicked it alive, and cried out again, "I ain't."

Clint shook his head, then looked up at the old man and the girl. "All you mountain folk just as slick as soap on a rope?"

The old man smiled. "All I did was read 'em from the Word. That's my job, boy."

"And I admire your guts, old man. You're lucky they're not all over the boardwalk." He looked up into the man's one good eye. "You were betting it'd work out like this."

"I was right, I guess."

"That Book," Clint said with an adrenal rush of anger he did not understand, "you *used* it to make peace."

The old prophet gave a grin wide enough to show the dentures. "Or it used me. Anyway, it's been used to make peace before. There's a verse that says—"

"I'll bet there is. But bottom line is that Jesus didn't save your little lamb. Wolves did that . . . We did that . . . I did that."

Oddly, the old man agreed. "Yes," he said, "you did that. And the lamb was saved."

"Thank you," mumbled the girl from the hamburger stand.

Backer smiled. "You townsfolk think outlaws from the past are romantic."

The girl tried to speak, but Backer cut her short. "But today we got Nam vets, we got misfits, we got psychos. And we're all pond scum to you straights. But as long as we got paper money, you'll swallow us. You might choke, but you swallow." He tossed a wad of cash between the preacher and the girl. It lay there, crumpled and dirty on the boardwalk.

"I still thank you," the girl said.

"Just common sense. Cozy little town here, but we're not colorful characters a hundred years dead. We're real and we're trouble. Too much trouble and we'd have to leave the playground before it's used up."

"Maybe it's time for you to stop playing," the preacher said.

Without answering, Clint turned his back and returned to Darby's.

━━━━━━

Four hours later Roper tilted his chair against the wall. "Cody's gun, huh?" he shouted over the jukebox din.

Pieces of the revolver were scattered over a cloth. The weapon was being assembled and lubricated by Colt with drug-rush concentration. "There was s'posed to be a paper with it . . . I forgot."

"Uh huh. Kept it in real fine shape too prob'ly. Replaced the barrel three times, the cylinder twice, and the stock once. Too bad about the paper."

"No . . ." Colt looked up, his pupils so small they had almost disappeared. "It was Cody's gun . . . I know."

Roper's chair legs hit the floor. "How you know?"

"Because . . ." With a final *click* the ancient .45 was together—nicked and scratched, but complete and shiny with lubrication. "Because . . ." Colt studied the gun's reflection in the mirror behind the bar. "Because Colonel Cody used this piece to kill people." He aimed at his own smiling image, squeezed the trigger, heard the hammer *snap!*

"This gun," he went on, "ain't afraid of death."

Ronda, Colt's woman since Clint brought him to the pack, nestled her dark head against his. "His big brother Clint learned him how to shoot." She ran her fingers through his thick brownish hair. "You're a big shot . . . with a gun."

As the day wore on, the bar shook with bikers, tourists, some curious locals, and Darby, who trotted to and fro mentally debating between shades of cream he would have on his new Pontiac after these maniacs were gone.

Clint Backer was involved in a poker game, made somewhat awkward by the red-tressed waitress, now seated among them, snoring softly with her head on the table.

Wulff was reminiscing about a run in New Orleans. Backer frowned as he threw in his jacks. That must have been five—six years ago? Those mounds of cartilage formed about his nose again as he estimated. He looked up in time to see the short silhouette of another waitress move through the neon glare in the Superburger across the street.

Spyder, Deacon, and Porky, forgiven by their leader for the afternoon's insurrection (after a swift blow from Wulff that brought each to his knees), studied their cards.

But Wulff, aware of everything, followed Backer's glance. "Ol' Backer," he chuckled, looking at his cards, "ol' Scout, ain't anything enough for you?"

Backer's reddish gaze whipped back to the table. "What's that supposed to mean?"

Frowning, Wulff rearranged his cards. "You got plenty quail right here—including our hostess." He picked up the head of the waitress by the roots of her hair.

"Too much horsin' around," she observed, and fell back unconscious.

"Call," Backer said, spreading his cards past the waitress' left ear. "Full house . . . queens high."

"It *is* a full house, ain't it?" Wulff nodded at the Superburger building, throwing in his own cards, as did the others.

Backer kept his eyes on the chips as he picked them up and stacked them on this side of the waitress.

"That ol' man—" Spyder began.

"Some kinda voodoo. Don't never fight voodoo." Porky blew out his orange-stubble cheeks. "They got the answers."

"And you can't have *all* the woman, can you, Backer?" Wulff asked as Clint kicked his chair back, threw down the cards, and walked through the smoke to the door.

"Out."

"We'll see, Ol' Scout." Wulff chuckled, looking directly through the window toward the neon of the Superburger. "We gonna see."

Clint Backer took his place in the burger stand line. When his turn came, the girl with the green eyes and the auburn bangs asked, without looking up from her order form, "Yes? C'mon, what's your pleasure?"

"You."

She saw him then. The pencil, held so primly, skittered off the page.

"Not me, please." Her green eyes held Backer's, and there was something there beyond her two decades of mountain life.

"Come out with me."

"No."

"On my machine." His fingers flicked back toward the Harley, parked at Darby's, and he was sincere.

"We'll just ride. I bet you ain't never felt the night wind on your face that way before."

She hesitated, looking through the glass.

A woman who, Clint thought, bore a striking resemblance to Lyndon Johnson squeezed her long press-on nails over the girl's shoulder.

"Time for your break, Lynne, babe."

Lynne hesitated.

"G'wan . . . I know how you young ones are when they got religion."

She pushed the younger girl aside and took her place at the window. Backer thought he detected a look of regret in those green eyes before they disappeared behind the grill.

"Now then . . ." Lyndon Johnson drawled, tearing out a fresh order sheet with her left hand while steadying harlequin glasses with her right, "what'll it be, young man?"

"Lessee." Backer scratched his jaw. "Well now . . ."

He looked up. "I got about two hundred friends, and they are *all* hungry." He watched the bustling figure at the rear of the shop.

"So . . . I guess you better make it about four hundred double cheeseburgers."

The harlequin glasses jerked up in protest, but Backer shoved two hundreds through the window. "Hold the onions . . . tightly."

She started to say something, snapped her jaw shut as her hand closed over the cash, and turned to holler in Spanish to the back of the shop.

"And would it be too much trouble to ask for extra sauce on seventy-three of those?"

She started to speak, but Backer cut her off. "You remind me a lot of my favorite aunt—Pearl. She's dead now."

Backer was behind the shop in time to see the green-eyed girl pump her short legs onto the pedals of a ten-speed.

Backer stood and watched her curl around a side street. Then the forest covered her.

"Good man," he yelled as he came back around the corner of the shop, "and hold the mayo, huh? Here's a little extra something for your trouble." Another hundred sailed beneath the window as he jogged up the mountain path.

The girl at the counter started to respond, pocketed the extra bill, and shouted to the kitchen in Spanish.

"I'll be back Tuesday week," Backer panted, trying to keep up with the mountain girl on her bike.

He followed a thin trail for five minutes until it forked, snaking into the forest. Kneeling, he plucked up a small leaf, indented with bike tread, on the left branch.

"Way to go, Cochise," he told himself as he ran into the darkening forest.

There . . . Up ahead the girl slowed, coasting though an open gate in a small churchyard.

Squint lines ran down Backer's face as he saw the voodoo man from that afternoon smile with his big dentures and lean on his rake. He stood before a steepled building that displayed more age than piety, at least to Backer's eyes.

The girl parked her bicycle beneath a stained-glass portrait of a gaunt man with a dark beard and entered. The old man raked a moment longer, then followed her.

Backer vaulted the spiked fence that surrounded the lot, then circled the building. There was no rear door on the chapel.

He steadied himself against a tombstone and crunched through the early-fallen leaves to the front.

Just as Backer expected, the old man stood in the doorway.

"Let me in."

"Nope."

"You can't stop me."

"I don't suppose."

"Get out of my way and go to Hell."

"Not one or the other, boy. He don't want *you* there either."

"I want that woman."

"And He wants you." The old man rubbed his forehead with the back of a corduroy sleeve. "'Course, He wants *all* of us . . . but I just got a feelin' He means to have you."

Heat lightning flashed off the crude stained-glass windows and the old man's artificial left eye. "Got an idea you don't have much time left to decide." He stepped aside.

Dimly, Backer could see the girl kneeling at the far end of the little sanctuary.

"Come in then, son . . . if you want to meet *Him*."

Cursing, Backer turned away and staggered down the trail.

━━━━━

After sundown there was a different feel to the town. The streets were full, the two bars and the liquor store feeding a continuous stream of weekend visitors and locals.

Music blared from passing vehicles, everything from Dylan to old Hank Williams stuff.

Smoke and clatter crowded Darby's. Clint pushed through the dancers and flattened himself against the bar.

"Drink."

"What'll it be?"

Backer pointed at the bottle in the man's hand. "That. All of it."

He took the bottle and a glass and elbowed his way across the floor to a table that already contained two girls (townies, by the look of them) and three bikers.

"Backer, ol' Scout."

"'Lo, tall dark and ugly," another biker said.

"Move."

"Huh?"

"I knew they were pigs," one of the locals whispered.

"Ol' Scout, you be lean and mean Second Rider, but—" the biker next to Backer blustered.

Clint picked him up and held him. "Move over there or get thrown. It's your vertebrae."

"Okay!"

Someone handed Backer a clay pipe, and he sucked at it without comment, passed it on without looking.

"Runnin' on empty?" Spyder smirked.

Carefully Clint put down the bottle—the glass had long since become logistically impossible—and eyed the biker over its rim.

"Little Spyder, run on very quiet feet, or I squash you all flat now."

Wulff's glove was suddenly curled over Backer's shoulder. Backer flinched. "Make *noise* when you move, like a normal man."

Laughing in his throat, Wulff sat opposite Backer. "What normal man could control this army of yahoos?"

Backer nodded. "Okay . . . So give me a hit of whatever that is."

The water pipe crossed the table without a sound save for its gurgling. Backer followed it with a chaser from the bottle.

"You missed her, huh?"

Backer shook his head, long hair flickering about the high cheekbones.

"Backer . . ." Wulff squeezed the drunken biker's shoulder. "Even I—even you can't have *everybody*."

Backer backed up, took Wulff by his thick wrist, and slowly forced his arm to the table.

"Sometimes you're just stupid," Wulff said in his throat, one wide palm up on the table.

"Sometimes it's win or die," Clint said, and he released Wulff's hand, grabbed the bottle, and wobbled from the bar.

You can't buy me, she had told Colt.

Miserable beyond understanding, disgusted with the greed of the town, and annoyed with the attitude of the pack, Backer leaned against the building corner and watched the waitress close up. Her short figure moved back and forth, then the lights went out in the burger joint one by one.

Backer's joint was only a glowing ember as he flung it into the gutter and watched the girl lock the door and fasten the ten-speed to the carrier on a green Volkswagen.

His big black Harley wheeled into the street, lights out.

Following the green Volkswagen, they drove through town and up a side trail, then down a black mountain track.

Coasting most of the way, he watched the VW cut left off the road and stop next to a cabin set among the pine branches. The VW's high beams went off.

Clint straddled his hog, watching from the darkness as the girl unlocked the door, hitting the lights from room to room.

There are no important people.

He finished the last of the stuff left in his bottle while watching her eat a bowl of yogurt over the kitchen sink. He couldn't see what color yogurt it was, but he saw the butterfly decals on the walls around her, the notes plastered to the refrigerator. Somehow it all angered him. *Home. Even here there's a home . . . for one snippy brunette . . . probably makes minimum wage . . .*

You can't buy me.

Maybe I can freak your head a little, townie.

Clint always told his women, "It's only good when it's mutual." He never tried seduction, he had contempt for bullies. But this time . . . a little circus act, a little fright for the praying, pious Hamburger Pattie. An example of the real world's hard edges.

Open up new horizons for you, sweetie, the whiskey and the hash in him whispered as he padded across the road and watched her progress through the cabin to the bedroom window. She flicked the light, entered the bathroom, closed the door.

Backer circled the house. One bedroom. One car. He pressed his face against the living room window, saw a small yellow couch, a basket chair, some ferns. She lived alone and wasn't expecting company.

The telephone was on a stand in the corner, beneath a wall-mounted cross. Only one phone too—he'd bet Aubrey's money on it. There hadn't been one in the kitchen or bedroom. No need in a place this small.

Drunkenly moving a few paces back, he tripped on a stone, fell painlessly on his side, chuckled.

In the bedroom the girl's hairbrush froze. She listened, reminded her self to check the locks.

Still laughing, Backer got up, shook away the dust, took a running leap, and plunged through the glass of the living room window.

The girl screamed as he flopped and rolled, his boots tangled in the telephone cord.

Glazed eyes furrowed in concentration, he got both hands on the cord and ripped it from the wall.

She stood in the hallway, wrapped in a shapeless white nightgown and fuzzy bunny slippers, frozen. Then she screamed again, flinging the hairbrush at him.

Purely by luck he caught it. "My hair must look a sight," he mocked.

She swiveled and ran, slamming the bedroom door.

Dropping the brush, Backer continued the endless task of disentangling himself from the phone cord.

There. Now . . . Oops. He fell. *Still have to navigate.* He pulled himself up by the bedroom doorknob as the girl, hearing it rattle, darted left, then right. A hiding place . . . a weapon.

Nothing.

"Run, l'il white bunny rabbit," Backer urged, putting a foot though the door paneling above the knob. "Run hard."

Losing his balance, he fell to his knees and climbed up again, listening to the sound of the girl drag the wicker laundry hamper from the bathroom and wedge it beneath the knob.

"We were—were made for each other. You're cute, and I'm not."

The bedroom door split loose from the latch, the hamper spilling clothes over the floor as Backer sprawled onto the bed.

Whirling into the bathroom, the girl slammed and locked the door.

Suddenly tired, Backer flopped over the bed's yellow satin coverlet. Liking it, he plucked up folds and rubbed them against his hot skin.

A box of mints lay open on the bedside table, and he delicately took one and swallowed it. The tinfoil had not been removed, and he grimaced as it went past his molars.

Inside the bathroom, the girl balanced herself on the edge of the tub, knocked loose the window screen, and tried to squeeze herself through the narrow aperture.

Backer slammed the bathroom door open and saw one bunny slipper drop back into the tub as the girl ran away from the cabin and into the darkness of the pines.

Flapping at the coverlet that still enshrouded him, Backer tripped to the front door, staggered to his Harley, and flung the coverlet away. It flew into the night like a large yellow bat.

His bike growled into life on the first kick, and he twisted the bars so the headlamp's glow lit the branches across the road.

He blinked. Mighty thick in there. He shrugged. He was a fox, she was a rabbit. Rolling into the woods, he opened the accelerator and raced after the sounds of the running woman.

With a stop so sudden that she fell, taking a mouthful of earth, the girl realized that she should have taken the road, tried for the town. Ahead there was only a gorge spanned by a rope-and-plank bridge and wilderness beyond.

The Harley growled behind her.

Narrowing her eyes, she clambered up and ran barefoot for the bridge.

Viciously whipped by pine needles stabbing at him out of the dark, the rider wobbled through the forest. Then his high beam lit up the bridge and the empty gorge below. His brakes shrieked and the machine skidded, stopping at the lip of the ditch.

Caught in the motorcycle's light, the girl balanced at the center of the suspension bridge. She held a dry branch overhead. Even under *her* weight the old boards groaned.

"You can't make it," she called to him as the bridge swayed. "And if you do, you'll drop." Her green eyes flicked down to twenty feet of darkness and an empty, muddy gully.

The branch drooped in her hands as she tried to maintain her balance.

"Nobody's that crazy," she yelled.

"There ain't nonesuch, is there?" He pulled back and with a shake of his head found himself staring at three bridges and three determined girls in white, each a mouse ready to swat a wolf.

"Lady," he said, gunning his machine, "I admire your attitude."

The Harley shrieked forward. Which bridge? He aimed at the one in the center of his triple vision, felt the old wood take the weight as he jumped onto it.

There was a tearing shriek, and a rope split. The bridge swung.

"Give it up!" the girl cried, clinging to the remaining hand cable. "I'm protected! Go away!"

"There are no important people." Backer swayed on his bike, then tried to jerk up the front end and move forward.

There was a howling as the old planks split beneath his front tire and the big machine dipped into space. The rider was thrown over his own handlebars, hit the edge of the writhing bridge, grabbed at the snapping rope, felt it coil around his throat, and then all at once was still, twirling by his neck in the night wind, twenty feet up as the bike's front wheel sunk through the bridge, raged and growled, and became as still as the rider.

Tears ran down the girl's face as she inched hand-over-hand back across the bridge wreckage, holding tight to the unsplit side of the rope.

Then she was next to the steaming Harley and the rider dangling down into the gorge.

He gurgled as she inched past the bike. She stopped. "Hang there!" She looked down into the gorge where he hung, face blue in the moonlight.

"Ohhhh . . ."

Holding to the remaining cable, she squatted and gave a swat at the rope which was squeezing the life out of the rider.

The hemp unwound, and Backer pitched headlong into the blackness.

"No—"

She heard him splat into the muddy sand.

Carefully, on hands and knees, she dragged herself to the safety of the bank, rolled over, and lay there facing the stars, wheezing.

From the ditch below came a groan.

Rolling over, her fingers digging into the bank, she saw the rider below, facedown in mud, gagging.

The choking stopped.

Weeping, she wriggled her way down the side of the bank, lost her hold, and tumbled through the mud to the body of the dying biker.

Taking a breath, she sat up, gripped his shoulders, and pushed-rolled him over.

Dead . . . Or nearly.

She ran her finger through his mouth, flung out the clay. Then she used her upper-body strength to rock back and forth, shaking him.

He fell back, lifeless.

Grimly, she put her mouth on his, began breathing for him. She crossed her fingers on his chest and tried CPR.

There was a sudden explosion of mud and coughing as the rider took in air.

His head fell back in the soil, breathing normally now.

Eyelids flickering, lips moving feebly, he tried to form words. "What . . .?"

Her hand was on his chest as she leaned over his face. "What?"

"Your God . . ." he muttered, eyelids fluttering. "Your God can't help anybody."

The heel of her hand took him across the face, and then she sank back against the slippery wall of the gulch, alternately laughing and coughing.

——

Backer cracked open his swollen eyelids the following morning and saw his Harley suspended over him like a slaughtered hog. Yelping, he scrabbled away from its shadow and bumped against the girl.

Swollen-eyed, sniffling, she sat against the bank.

"What are *you* doing here?" he croaked.

"I . . . I came because I thought *He* wanted me to . . . and not just leave you to die."

"Don't give me that God jive! There ain't nonesuch!"

"There is. I was just as rotten and hungry as you. But I finally ran out of excuses. I was dying for answers. Really." A sad, secret little smile came and went. "During the school year—I'm a biology major—my philosophy teacher gave me a Bible . . . Somebody should give you one."

"Nobody gives anybody anything. All they do is bait the hook so they can reel you into the boat."

She leaned toward him, a small silver cross falling out of her mud-stained robe. "He didn't have to reel me in. I jumped. I found that Christ accepted me. He's paid for everything . . . even for what you tried to do to me last night. He paid with His own life."

"And a cold dead Christ is no better than a live bleeding one."

"He didn't *stay* dead."

Backer groaned, putting his head in his hands. "What does all that holy-roly stuff get you anyhow?"

She looked at him. "It got me here."

There was an ominous rumble, and the pair looked up to see the black rubber of bike tread jutting out over the lip of the gulch.

"Backer, ol' Scout, you don't miss *nothing*, do you?" Fuzzy-bearded Porky scrambled down the bank.

"Leave it lay."

The girl stood up, stared into Clint's eyes. "He didn't die for nothing," she said hoarsely, urgently. "He's alive. That power is walking this place right now."

Porky and Deacon hit the bottom of the gulch. "He'll get you *free*," she crackled.

"Hey!" Colt shouted from astride his Triumph at the gorge rim.

"Man," Porky said, reaching for her, "you don't let anything get away, do you, Scout?"

She flinched back into the wall of earth as riders hopped down.

Deacon took her arm. She pulled away, tried to climb, slipped down, and turned back to the wall, her hands full of mud. "That's all it is," she said simply to Clint, "mud and death. He dived under it and came back with life in His hands, all shiny and clean . . . for you. Can't you *see*?"

Almost, for the flicker of a second, he did see. There was a dirty, torn, bedraggled, desperate girl with bangs and a badly swollen nose, holding a handful of river bottom. And then his vision blurred and he saw a hot white-bright something held out to him by a muscled brown forearm, offering him—

Porky grabbed the girl's wrists. "You is U.S. Grade A, Hamburger Pattie."

There was a yelp and Porky was down, his thighbone nearly fractured by a kick from Clint.

"What's *with* you, man?" Porky clutched his leg, groaning.

"It ain't *all* your personal property," Spyder said, moving in with Deacon.

"I said leave it lay." Clint glanced at the girl. "Everybody. We all end up with what we started with."

"What was that exactly?" Porky asked as other riders pulled the group from the gorge.

"S' nothin, I think," Spyder said.

The bridge trembled beneath the tread of Godzilla, who nonchalantly lifted Backer's Harley and brought it back to safety.

"Backer . . ." He shook his head, bouncing the bike. "You gots to stop usin' things all up. I mean . . . this here's a *machine*." He lifted Clint onto the seat. Backer bit his lip as pain cut through him in a dozen places.

The machine trembled into life.

"It works," he mumbled, looking at the gauges.

"Yes," said the girl from behind him, "it does."

Without a glance or a word, Clint hit the throttle, lurched back on one wheel, and shot down the road.

The other riders followed, whooping, trying to match his speed.

All but Colt, who lingered, eyeing the girl over the handlebars of his Triumph.

"Sister, you must have something. You must reee-ly have something."

The girl watched him race away, and she fingered the silver cross that dangled from her neck.

"I do."

4

THE MOUNTAIN

"**S**weet Mama . . . Circus in town." Godzilla halted before the gaggle of state cars that jammed the streets as the group returned from the gulch.

"Meet you down the line," Colt muttered to Clint. Clint nodded, and Colt's Triumph was moving down the road before the group halted.

Wulff slouched against a motel balcony railing as a trooper pushed Backer aside to reach him.

"I surely do hate cops," muttered Backer, "or anybody else who tries to turn you into a gelding." His mother's worn face flashed through his mind. He shooed the image away.

The trooper handed a paper to his superior, who towered over the slouching Wulff. Bent over like that, naked to the waist, skin as white as an unhealed scar, Wulff looked about as dangerous as a lump of quartz. But Backer knew how quickly that could change.

"Here's the ten-twenty-four." The senior officer took the report.

Wulff rubbed sleep from his eyes, smiling peacefully.

"No warrants or wanteds," admitted the trooper, and Backer breathed a silent sigh of relief that Colt's ID wasn't on the sheet.

"All damage paid for, cash on the line. There *were* some complaints, but they've all been withdrawn." He glanced at Wulff with contempt. "You greased this town enough to slide it down the mountain."

Wulff shrugged. "Most people can be lubricated if you got the grease." He crumpled the empty Coors can in his fist, then tossed it expertly over his shoulder, where it tumbled off the balcony and bounced off the inside rim of a litter container shaped like a smiling raccoon.

"I am so glad you made that rim shot," said the trooper, "because if you pirates so much as litter the streets again, I'll put you inside until your chrome rusts. Do you copy that?"

"Okey-dokey, Smokey," yawned Wulff. He raised his large head and projected his voice over the rooftops. "Okay, Wolves, let's go someplace else!"

Colt joined the caravan outside of town, but it was many miles before Clint was spotted, veering in to take his place beside the leader.

———

Dealing and ingesting FaveRock drugs and spending FaveRock cash, the commando army of bikes and black-and-silver vans climbed the turreted face of Colorado.

At sunset their overheated engines sizzled to a stop in the silence of a primeval place called The Garden of the Gods. It was an unsullied wilderness area of rocky spires and towering pines.

Godzilla heaved his bulk from the saddle. "Party time," he grunted. "If I don't look out, I'm gonna catch me sober."

"Never that." Colt laughed, pulling alongside, Ronda seated behind him, her arms curled around his broad but thin shoulders, now covered in buckskin and fringe courtesy of a Red River tourist trap. He flapped his new black Stetson at her, urging her down.

"There's more to bein' a man than wearin' cowboy clothes," she mumbled, sinking beneath a rocky outcropping.

Spyder rumbled past. "You better not let Wulff catch you flashing that iron, little dude."

Colt grinned, continuing to twirl the old .45 as if he were a movie cowboy.

"Don't get uptight, Spyder-man. You don't scare me, and Wulff don't scare me." He laughed. "Why should I worry about old men like you guys?"

"Walk easy, Colter." Clint rolled alongside, speaking stiffly from a still-swollen face. "Just shut up now and then, so we know you're there by the silence."

Clint's head ached. The voice of the girl in the gulch, sniffling and wheezing, bounced against the sides and top of his skull.

"Don't tell me what to do! We're Wolves! We're free!" Colt shouted.

Be free . . . The power's here, right now . . .

The vans were pulled into a rough circle, and a massive bonfire crackled at its center as high-decibel rock blasted out over the popping flames.

"So let's go join the party," Colt urged.

Clint shook his head, and it was stuffed with pain and the sound of the girl's voice. "No . . . Not now."

"What else is there to do, man?" Angrily Colt kicked his Triumph alive, twisted the wheel toward the bonfire. "Party, man. What else is there?"

"I dunno," Clint answered, looking away into the shadowy thickets. "Something maybe . . . maybe."

"Now you sound like me, like you always make fun of." Colt's voice rose, ready to take either end of an argument on "the meaning of it all." "There's just these hills and us," he cried. "I finally got it figured. Just those greedy townies back there and us! Just the Wolves!" His gloved fingers gripped Clint's shoulder. "Just us, Clinton."

Clint looked down at his brother's hand. There was a gouge in the glove leather, and a bloody scab beneath.

Blood and mud and a tiny silver cross . . .

Colt looked at him oddly. "Your nerves are overheating, Clinton."

"We serve the Speed King," his older brother snarled. "All our nerves are hot. It's the occupational hazard, kid."

Colt shook his head, his face hidden by the wide brim of the Stetson. "Ahh, but you can't let anybody know that." He twirled the old gun Hollywood-fashion. "Keep 'em all on the run . . . Keep 'em afeared."

"Is everybody scared—deep inside, I mean?" Clint asked.

Colt chuckled. "Not us Wolves."

"Not even scared of dyin'?"

Again Colt laughed. "Death . . . he ain't no big number to do. Just like all the rest, you gotta make *him* afeared of *you*." He slipped the .45 into its holster. "Just keep your nerves packed in ice."

"My nerves are shakin'."

"For certain sure," Colt agreed. Then he pointed at

the forest. "And if Bambi came prancin' outta them woods, you'd jump like Jack Flash."

Gently Clint asked, "What makes you think Bambi would be on your side, little bro?"

"There's only one side," Colt answered impatiently, "your own. So let's go and party 'til we get dead."

"No!" Clint jerked his bike away, spraying dirt. His Harley grumbled into the dark wilderness.

A clod of dirt had struck Colt in the face. He rubbed it away and glanced at it.

When his startled gaze shot out from under the hat brim, he saw only the trees melting together in the evening.

Somewhere in there, twisting and turning, his older brother bumped through the dark, alone.

Briefly Colt listened to the fading bike, his fingers tracing along the edge of the black gun butt, then resting against the cartridge belt slung around his lean waist.

He started to hum to himself, a song the children at the institute had been taught.

"Jesus loves me, this I know—"

He stopped himself, turned toward the noise of the party at the bonfire.

At the edge of the circle Ronda slumped, covered by Deacon's arms.

"Let's you and me go, Gun," Colt said in a small boy's voice as he twisted the accelerator around as far as it would go, driving his wheels back to the pack.

———

His big machine resting quietly against a tree, Clint Backer knelt beside a pond, stars beginning to reflect in the

waters. He saw his reflection, the battered face, lines starting to grow around the mouth.

He picked up a stone, let it sink into the pond. Black
ripples spread outward and then the waters, a reflection of
the night sky, returned to glimmer beneath him.

"More," he whispered, "a body's just got to leave
more when he goes away."

———

The unmistakable screech of a bullet cut through the
party's uproar. Heads turned, eyes searching the shadows.

Antique .45 smoking in his fist, Colt stood atop a
van.

"Not much of a honcho, huh, Ronda?" He laughed
and, wheeling cat-quick, sent another shell spitting from
the barrel of the old revolver and into the night. A Coors
can exploded, foam cascading down a rock.

"Hey hey hey!" Spyder shouted drunkenly. "Go,
Buffalo Backer!"

"Easy duty, brave comrades." Colt waved the
weapon. "You just points the mighty fire stick and . . . does
it!" Swiveling and firing in the same moment, splinters of
bark flew from a tree across the clearing, splattering onto
Porky who slouched beneath.

"See . . . Clint taught me . . . At home . . . Back before
they—before they—"

"Hey! Shut it down or I'll stuff that cannon down
your crazy throat," cried Porky.

Giggling, Colt fired another slug into the tree, inches
above Porky's head.

Twisting, firing, the glistening gun barrel spat flame, shots sizzling through the camp. Riders ducked, cursing as Colt put in more shells.

Suddenly Roper's lean form was outlined against the yellow-red fire. "Chill it out now, little Backer brother. That's permanent death you're dribbling."

The old black .45 moved slowly until it hovered before Roper. A slow smile crawled across Colt's white face.

"It is, ain't it?" he said softly. "Death, right here inside this little black tube . . . Death in a hole."

The barrel swung upwards into his own face. "The power of life and death in my hand."

Roper reached for the gun. The barrel jumped around to point directly at Roper's heart.

The gaunt biker froze.

"Looky there," Colt whispered wonderingly, "what a teeny piece of Death does even to you, good ol' fearless ol' Rope."

Roper stood very still.

"I ain't afraid of dyin'," Roper muttered.

Colt laughed, high, hysterical.

"I'm not! I just . . . just . . ."

"Just what, Rope my friend . . . my family . . . my fearless other brother?"

"I just don't want to die . . . for nothing."

"So my very old friend Roper is scared out of his very old jeans by my new friend Mister Death. Tccch and poo!"

He turned to the mob below him, clustered around the van. "What about you guys? Mister Death your friend? Huh?" His finger twitched, and a bullet sped over their heads. The crowd flinched back, leaving Colt alone in the firelight.

"All this time I watched you guys ride with death. I mean, don't we? We ain't afraid. That's the whole point . . . just the whole and only point we got . . . ain't it?"

The bonfire hissed in the silence of the night.

"So how come you and Mister Death ain't really friends after all? Ever since Clint roared up and took me to you . . . you been lyin'?"

Wulff pushed to the front of the pack. "That's all, man. You're done."

"Forget it, Wulff." The old .45 pointed at the leader's head.

———

From way back in the trees, Backer snubbed out the butt of his Marlboro, aware of the sudden silence. Then a familiar voice traveled along the wind.

"*Colt—*" he cried, rising, pushing through the branches, stumbling in the dark. There was the camp, and the fire, and the crowd . . . and someone on top of a van, framed against the moon . . .

He knew.

"Colll-t!"

"Clint, can you get behind this?" Colt called as Backer shoved through the pack. "These guys are *afraid* . . . Of me! . . . Me and my friend Mister Death. All this time I been tryin' to be not afraid, like you. Tryin' to be on the *inside*."

"Colter, *please*—" He was almost through the crowd now.

"Ever since you brought me to the pack, I been tryin'

to be like them. Different from those bozos out there. Not afraid of nothin'. But *look* at these guys."

He sent another bullet flying over the heads of the crowd. Shouts and screams.

"See? Just as cold and scared and empty as me. See Clinton? They can't help. Who could help me, I wonder. Not them. Look at their eyes!"

Backer got to the van. He reached up, pulling at his brother's leg. "Colt, I'll take care of you, kid—"

"Can't wait no more, man. I gotta show 'em what I learned . . . Death, he ain't no big thing, man. No big thing at all."

Colt leaned over, put his hand on his brother's knuckles. "See?"

The barrel of the old gun went into his mouth. The back of his head came off . . .

5

THE CONTINENTAL DIVIDE

Another dawn . . . a shallow grave. During the night the caravan moved south, to the place chosen by the Scout. They had ridden slowly, a string of lights drifting down the slopes . . . with an empty socket of darkness between the headlamp of the Second Rider and the following machine.

Now they stood before the unmarked grave . . . More than unmarked—the dirt had been smoothed and covered with brush. Backer stood at one side, Wulff on the other, the pack around them.

"You gonna speak over him, Wulff?" Roper asked.

"You're the leader," Godzilla agreed. "You oughta give him his—what they call 'Last Rights.'"

The pack nodded. Wulff cleared his throat.

They waited.

"Well, Colt was . . ."

Backer watched the red-tinged clouds drift on the horizon. They were reflected in the red slits of his eyes.

"G'wan, Wulff," Godzilla urged, "tell us how we got his body committed in the ground, an' it's okay in a surely certain hope of the resurrection an' the like . . . the way ol' Father Hansen usta do when we was kids."

Wulff shifted his weight, the black leather on his big shoulders creaking. "Colt was . . . he . . . we remember him because . . ."

More silence, and the wind whipped against them.

"You got nothing to say." Backer turned away, moved toward the bikes. "You just got nothing to say, Wulff."

"Hey!" Porky shouted. "What about his machine?"

Colt's golden Triumph stood beyond the grave, glinting in the sun.

"His old lady Ronda drove it up here, but she don't need it," Deacon called, putting his arm over the girl's shoulders.

"Yours now, I guess, Backer," Wulff said from across the grave.

"Don't need two bikes." Backer swung aboard his Harley.

"But it's *yours*, man."

Reaching over and ripping the key from the Triumph, Backer muttered, "It wasn't mine. Colt wasn't mine. I brought him to the pack, and the pack took him. Here!" He flung the keys at the foot of the grave.

Wulff made no move to take them. He stared at Backer, an odd look forming beneath his thick black brows.

"It's all there is to remember him by," Ronda said.

"It's like his estate," cried Spyder. "Let's all take a piece of it!"

"Right." Deacon flipped open a toolbox. A silver wrench spun through the air and smacked into Porky's palm.

"Something for everybody."

Wrenches, pliers, hammer. The pack descended on the Triumph.

Clint turned away, watching the clouds redden in the rising sun.

When they were done, there was an oil spill on the ground where the golden machine had been.

Deacon nuzzled Colt's girl, the chrome sissy bar in his hand. The Triumph's grease-covered chain dangled from Ronda's fingers.

"Here!" A shiny sphere flashed through the sun. Backer reached out and caught the Triumph's headlamp.

"Thought you might want it," Wulff said.

The silver lens gleamed up from Backer's palm.

"Ol' Colt belongs to the pack now, for always." Wulff smiled.

"How does he taste?" Backer asked, staring down at the lamp.

"Everybody tastes the same to the worms." Wulff shrugged. "And there was nothing else to do. We're all goin' his direction."

"We're already there." With all his strength, Backer swiveled and sent the headlamp sailing over the mountain-side. It spun and twisted a long time before disappearing.

———

The gang elbowed for space in a Pueblo bar.

Backer sat at the side of the counter, staring out the window.

"Whattaya think he'll come back as?" Ronda asked, licking beer foam from her lips.

"Colt ain't comin' back. He's dead," Godzilla told her sadly.

"Talkin' about reincarnation, Godz," Deacon said. "Getting reborn."

"Can you do that?"

"Me, I'm gonna come back as the noise a beer can makes when you pop it open." Roper sighed. "Always appealed to me."

"Can you do that?" Godzilla asked.

"Where do you think Colt is, really?" Ronda pulled away from Deacon.

"Doin' wheelies on God's main drag." Deacon reached for her.

"Who is God, I wonder," Ronda muttered, letting Deacon take her in his arms again.

"Whatever people want most." He laughed.

"That's sex, I guess."

"Money, man," Porky countered, "the Almighty Dollar."

"I'd like a dog," Godzilla put in. No one heard him.

"Getting high is most everything," Roper said.

"So God is whatever gets you highest . . . Dope, chicks, bread."

"Then," Spyder concluded, "High is God." He licked the foam from his lips.

Ronda reversed it and giggled. "God is high."

"None of you can read it," Deacon said. "Since God is whatever you want most, what Colt really wanted came and got him."

"What *is* this trip, man?" Wulff growled abruptly.

"Simple." Deacon shrugged. "Death, man. Colt wanted it, he got it. Everybody gets it. Death is god."

The bar was suddenly quieter. Shannon grabbed her drink.

"Ahh, ol' Colt wasn't afraid of nothin'," Ronda said. "He proved that. He's right up there in Heaven with the Big Bopper and Buddy Holly and Buddha and Jesus."

"I'll tell you where Colt is," Wulff snarled, slamming down his mug. "He's forty miles away under six feet of Rocky Mountain dirt. He's dead. Now shut up about it."

A moment's silence, then Roper asked, "What do you think, Clint?"

Backer got to his feet from a table in the corner. "I think you're all just about dead." He removed the packet of drug money from inside his jacket, dropped it into the jug of beer, and swung the pitcher over the bar. It hit the mirror viciously. Liquid spilled over the riders as cracks snaked across the glass. Backer waited for a response, but no one moved. He stood in front of Wulff, paused, then slammed open the door and left.

There was no sound in the bar but the dripping of the beer down the shattered mirror while the pack listened to Backer's Harley start up and rumble off. Wulff stood at the bar staring out the dirty window, watching Backer race up the mountain road until the rider was out of sight.

———

Backer shot through Pueblo. His brother's last words and his maddened, hungry face twisted and melded with other words, other faces.

All the time I was trying to get in—

He accepted me. Somebody should give you a Bible—

Ignoring a stop sign, he skidded past a semi and looked up to see a station wagon full of children, inches away. He veered violently, jumped a curb, grazed a light pole, hit a shopping cart, and crashed against a wall.

Blackness.

Voices. Curses.

"Is he—"

"Look at the blood. Better call—"

"Drunken scumbags. Not safe for—"

Eyes open, creased against the glare. He pushed away the weight of the bike, grabbed a light pole, pulled himself to his feet, rubbing blood from his eyes. The blue glare coalesced into a flickering neon sign.

Bread Bookstore. Bibles.

"Don't try it by yourself. Let me help."

Still squinting against the blood running down his face into his eyes, he saw the silver cross hanging from the man's neck. The man looked like someone he should know.

"There's a couch in the back room. You can lie down until the ambulance—"

Dragged into the shop. Crosses. Hands. Voices.

"No!" he screamed, pushing. A pyramid display of books toppled.

"You can't make it alone."

All those crosses spun in the lights.

"Let me help you."

LetmehelpLetmehelpLetmehelp—

They can't help. Look at their eyes—

Somebody should give you a Bible—

He stumbled through the shop. "Help me. Help me. Help . . ."

Suddenly his head was clear. Books were scattered about him. The young man with the cross waited.

"I can help you."

Angrily Backer thrust out his hand, ripped the cross from the man's neck.

"Is . . . this . . . anything? Is this anything?"

"It's everything."

Still clutching the emblem, Backer pushed/stumbled to the door. He sagged, put a hand on a glass-topped counter to steady himself. He looked down, focused. There was a thick Book inside the counter. He squeezed his fingers shut and sent his fist ramming down through the glass. More blood.

Lifting his lacerated hands, Bible in one, cross in the other, he said, "If it's not"—he flung the cross at the other's feet—"I'm gonna come back here and kill you."

He shoved the Bible inside his jacket and staggered out into the parking lot.

"It's been tried," the man said as Backer hauled his Harley upright, kicked it into life, and left smoking rubber on the asphalt, seconds before the arrival of the squealing patrol car.

———

Down Highway 87, past Evergreen and Boulder . . . Rock walls towered over him in Boulder Canyon, and still Backer rode.

High above the little town of Nederland, when the overheated machine could not continue, he parked in the shadow of a rocky outcropping and climbed, scrabbling with fingers and feet.

He pulled himself upward until his legs were flames of pain and his hands were numb. Then, rolling over a stone ledge, he rose to his knees and looked down over the hills.

A long time he knelt there, the wind lashing his hair. At last he collapsed back against a stone and stared.

Eventually he felt the Book's heavy weight dragging at his jacket. Without looking, he plucked it forth, dropped it to the earth.

It flopped open. The wind riffled the pages. The sun beat down on the words.

If a man keep my sayings, he will never see death.

He reached out and slammed the Book shut.

He opened it again.

I am come that you might have life.

The sun crossed the heavens; stars studded the black mountain sky. He slept without knowing it. Morning came, and he was reading again.

Come unto me.

"No."

Come.

He stood, then sagged as the pain shot up his legs.

"Are You?"

The hills of morning rolled away beneath him, and the wind died.

"If . . . if You are . . . I want to know!"

Silence.

Raising his torn fists he croaked, "In the Name of God, *is anybody out there?*"

"Heads up!"

Something slapped into the side of his face, then bounced off. He flinched, fingers going to face as a white blur went by him.

"We hit 'im, Daddy! Right in the face! Luke did it!"

"No sir! The wind did it! And it wasn't us that banged him up like that, honest!"

A white hound snatched the rubber ball in its teeth and trotted back to the two children.

"What are you guys *doing*? Intrusion, commere!" A big black man climbed over the top of the hill. The hound galloped over.

"Sorry, man." He took the ball from the dog's teeth and ran his fingers absently through the hound's white fur. "Don't run into many people this high up." He gazed at Backer's battered face.

"You had lunch?" he inquired abruptly.

"Ain't had breakfast." Backer felt his jaw for loose teeth.

"Got us a Winnebago . . . couple miles down . . . plenty of burgers. Restitution for the assault of the red rubber ball. Though I hope we—"

"No, Daddy!" the older boy blurted. "We didn't do *that*—"

"Hush, oracles." The big man put a hand over each young face. ". . . We got bandages too, and iodine."

"I'm fine."

"Sure you are. And hamburgers are better." He turned away. "C'mon, vandals, let's go masticate." Over his shoulder he added, "I'm Leon Kobol. The maniac munchkins are Luke and Jeremy." He started back down. "You can join us if you please."

Backer stared after them, rubbing his fingers against the sting along his jaw. Suddenly he shrugged and followed the three down the hill.

Bright red and white, the camper squatted in amongst the aspens.

"The family estate," Kobol said as they tumbled down the slope. "Or in the well-used words of Tony Curtis, 'Yonder lies da cast-el of my fodder.'"

"Worst impression I ever heard," Backer was forced to comment in spite of the pain in his head.

"Obviously limited experience on your part," the black man said, lumbering into the van and handing out barbecue instruments.

"There's *lots* worser impressionists than Daddy," Luke said proudly.

Kobol hopped out, dumped a battered bag of charcoal briquettes on the grill. "Hamburgers up momentarily. You like yours charred, charred, or charred?"

"Yeah." Backer stumbled, slumped down against a rock.

"You okay?"

"Fine . . . dandy." Backer slumped back against the rock. "Just hot."

"Yeah. Cold nights though." Kobol stripped off his shirt and hulked over the fire. "Luke, fetch the first aid kit, huh?"

"Not unless it's to doctor that meat," Backer protested. "All I need is a couple aspirin. Just . . . hot." He unzipped his jacket, tossed it aside. The Bible flopped out.

The chef quickly glanced away from the grill. "Yours?"

"I stole it. You got aspirin?"

Kobol said no more as Luke toddled over with the tablets, a jug of bottled water, and a Styrofoam cup.

Backer chugged back the pills, ignoring the cup.

"Yuk," said Luke, wiping the rim of the bottle with his sleeve.

"Hush, child . . . You can't judge wild animals like

you would a human being." Kobol flipped a steaming burger onto a bun.

"You live up here?" Jeremy asked, staring into Backer's eyes.

"Three miles southwest." Backer sighed, closing his eyes.

"What town izzat?"

"It's a chopper. Left it against a tree."

"A chopper is a motorcycle, Daddy," Luke said.

"Thanks so much, Walter Cronkite." Then, a moment later, "You . . . live on a hog?"

"Finances permitting." Backer looked at the grill. "Those things ain't gonna get no better."

"Here." Kobol plopped some burgers onto plates. "Let's eat 'em before they rot in the sun."

Backer stabbed at the lump on his paper plate with a plastic fork. The fork broke, and Backer picked up the hot patty in his fingers, gobbled it.

"Whose turn?" Luke asked.

"Mine, seems like." Without a glance at the gobbling rider, Kobol closed his eyes and said a quick blessing.

"Amen," said the family, Luke adding, "Bet I don't get sick this time, Daddy."

"But they're still not as good as Mommy's," Jeremy said with a full mouth.

"Never that. Just keep it inside you this time, huh?"

The meadow whirled around Backer. He shut his eyes again, and Colt's face was there.

"Your old lady split on you?" he asked to dispel the vision.

"She . . . died."

"Hard times."

"She's with Jesus." Jeremy wiped his chin.

"Sure she is, kid." Response to a small boy. Flickers of Colt at the same age, blows from their stepfather, Clint pushing in, taking the slaps meant for Colt. *I'll take care of you, kid—*

"Well, she is *so*," Jeremy said with a child's persistence. "Even if you don't believe it."

"None of my business what you believe, boy."

"Is," Jeremy insisted. "Jesus took her so she wouldn't hurt anymore."

"He doesn't want you to hurt either, mister," Luke added quietly.

"Maybe we should pray for this ugly man, Daddy."

The rider's eyes snapped open. He clutched the Bible, tossed it at Kobol. It was caught.

"That Book—you happen to know about that Book?"

The little charcoal grill hissed. Kobol paused. "A little something."

"Like, what do you know?"

"I know who it's about. Know Him personal."

"Yeah?"

"It's about Jesus Christ. He's the Man."

"We belong to Him," Jeremy said.

"We're Christians." Kobol looked up, grinned, went back to the meat.

"I'll be damned," Backer managed to say before he finally passed out.

"Possible negatory on that." Kobol left Luke to watch the grill while he reached into the the first aid kit.

———

By evening Backer had ripped off the bandages applied so delicately by Kobol. The rider's face was a mottled blue and green in the twilight.

A practiced hand touched his brow.

"At least your fever's down," Kobol said.

"Head's better."

"Sure it is." Kobol squatted while the children raced with the dog. "It just ain't on straight."

For a moment Backer stared at him. The black man chewed a stick with unconcern.

"Everywhere I go," Backer began, "it's . . . like He—It—I dunno . . . Something's hunting me."

Kobol nodded. "You're reaching up and He's reaching down."

"Who? Krishna? Lao-Tse? John Lennon and the walrus?"

Kobol chomped the stick. "Don't ask questions if you're gonna make up your own answers. Makes you look stupid."

"Excuse the hell out of me."

Taking the twig from his mouth, Kobol snapped it between his fingers. "And don't swear so much. It grieves me."

"You're pushin' your luck, new friend."

Absently Kobol yawned, his chest expanding massively.

Backer snapped a knuckle against the other man's swelling pectorals. "Nice display of meat on hook."

"Beg pardon?"

Shrugging his heavy trapezius, Backer muttered, "I ain't exactly shy in the anatomy department either. But that wouldn't be enough to keep you on your feet in *my* jungle, Christian."

Kobol smiled widely, displaying a golden tooth among the white. "The fact that I am the most impressive physical specimen God ever created fails to move you?"

"There's places I go, you come in packin' nothin' but muscle, they'll rip your hide off like a baseball with loose stitches. So push it not."

Kobol flung away the fragments of twig. "I never push what rolls by itself. But get this—" He leaned forward, and the gold tooth glistened. "What I know can be verified with as good a record as you can find. And when you get it, you generally know you got it." He yawned again. "Can you pronounce 'empirical'?"

"That upwardly-urban jive must go down real smooth with your ambitious black brothers, but it slices no ice in the jungles *I* come out of."

"Worked okay in some rice paddies I waded out of."

"The Nam?"

"Was a medic. Part of me's still there."

"The tooth?"

"Lost that in a dispute over poker etiquette in basic. *This* I left north of Saigon." He did something to his right eye. "'If thy right eye offend thee—'"

Backer coughed.

Kobol was flipping his glass right eye in his palm. "'Let us reason together,' eye to eye." His empty socket ogled the rider.

"Amusing as pie." Backer paused. "Seems I met somebody else with a glass eye . . ."

"Getting to be a fashion statement. Kids think I'm talented."

"I think you're a few bricks shy of a load and you're gonna tell me there were no atheists in foxholes."

"Dunno if there was or not. Nobody sported labels.

Either you wore your dog tags slung around your neck or thrust between your rigid dead teeth."

"So you flew back holy."

"Whole but not holy. Flew back courtesy of Uncle Airways with two purples and a smack habit big enough to tear up a city in a Japanese monster flick."

The eye popped back in, and Kobol got up. "Time to load up."

As they packed the Winnebago, Backer heard it all: Kobol's attempt to prostitute his wife; her refusal; her Christianity. A fight that ended with a blow.

"Must've hit her head on the coffee table. Found her in the emergency room. Begged her not to die."

Backer saw Colt with the gun in his mouth. *Death ain't no big thing . . .*

"'We forgive you,' she said. I *knew* she was talkin' about Jesus Christ. Then her eyes were looking at something . . . and she . . . went . . . someplace else."

"So you sentenced yourself to religion for life."

Kobol shook his head. "Think what you want. There never were any charges pressed, but I could've taken a sentence. What I couldn't handle was being forgiven."

"Easy exit for two-thirds of a wife-killer."

"That's the point, man. See? What I had coming, I had coming. But Jesus . . . He just took the guilt and walked away with it."

Backer's arm snapped out, slapped against Kobol's chest. "How do you handle it here—knowing there's no way what's happened will ever change—how do you live with yourself?"

"Because He lives inside me. Don't you get it, man? . . . Inside *I am full*." All the gear lashed, the children asleep inside the RV, Kobol swung open the cab.

"Maybe . . . Maybe." Backer shook his head. "I just . . . I can't get . . . all the way."

Kobol stopped with the door half-open, looked up with a frown on his face. "I will kick myself for this in the morning, but . . . why don't we go down and get your hog, and you come kick back at my place a while. After the time I told you about, I went back to school on the GI Bill. C.U., in Boulder. I'm a draftsman. Got a cabin a ways up the canyon. Still take a few classes. You could lay up and heal a while, meet some guys I know whose heads are on straight."

"You don't even *know me*."

Kobol nodded, sliding into the driver's seat. "Only relevant thing you've said today." He started up the engine. "Come or go, man. I got no more time to mess around with some beat-up white boy." The RV slid into gear.

"This is crazy."

"Yeah." He let up on the brake, and the Winnebago slid forward. "Train's pulling out."

Cursing himself through bruised lips, Backer made a grab for the door, bounced along a few feet, and fell off into the dirt. He was picking himself up painfully when he heard the brakes slam.

"I likes a man who knows his mind," Kobol said cheerfully, lifting the rider to his feet.

THE CABIN

*I*n the final event, Backer was returned to his abused Harley. Assuring the draftsman of his capability, he followed the camper back to the Boulder Canyon cabin. They arrived late, and Backer helped carry in the sleeping children, then unrolled his own sleeping bag by the living room couch.

"Sorry we got no guest suite," Kobol said, turning off the lights.

"Me too. I'm used to the finer things in life."

"Get past Go, collect two hundred dollars, and then you land on Luxury Tax." Kobol yawned. "Ain't it just the way, though."

But an hour later Clint still found himself staring at the low ceiling, unable to sleep.

Look at their eyes, man—
I was just as rotten and hungry as you—
The power's here—

He felt his bruised and aching mind begin to recover from shock—due, he knew, more than a little to the gentle but definite ministrations of the ex-Nam medic.

Finally he turned away from the sleep that would not come, switched on a lamp, and began flipping the pages of the Bible.

When Kobol went to the kitchen for breakfast, he found the rider, red-eyed and pale, sitting beside a steaming cup of coffee, still reading the Book.

"I don't think you can afford to wait," Kobol muttered sleepily. "Soon as I get someone to sit with the kids, let's you and me ride that hog of yours into town. Guess you need to talk to someone 'sides me, masterpiece that I am." He glanced at the calendar. "And school starts today."

They drove through the rain into Boulder and onto the Colorado University campus. Even in a hippie town, Backer's bruises and haunted expression got him second looks.

"Park in front of that building," Kobol hollered into the wind.

Backer swerved hard left, sending a gaggle of students and their papers flying.

"I meant when you could, man."

"I hit nobody," Backer shouted back.

Kobol's sigh brushed the back of the rider's neck. "Let's get you in and civilized before you snuff someone who might object."

It was a square stone building, smelling of old books and young students. Backer clomped up the stairs after Kobol.

Before they had reached the third-floor landing, Kobol stopped and turned.

"Do you absolutely have to make that much noise with those boots?"

"Yeah," Backer shrugged, "I guess."

"Then make noise *quietly*," Kobol whispered.

They opened the door on the tail-end of a philosophy class. An angry debate was going on.

"But Hume says—"

"Ahh, Socrates said it better first."

"Maybe. But *you* haven't."

Though most of them were seated, or as close to seated as a twenty-year-old gets, Clint, standing at the back, got the impression of a pack of small dogs trying to bring down a very wise, very amused old stag.

The venison in question was a bushy-haired instructor, vest buttoned incorrectly, who seemed to be smiling beneath his *bandido* mustache as the young hounds bayed.

"Good of you to credit Hume, Ronn," the old man said. "I believe you failed to footnote that particular little gem on your last blue book. A good beginning to the semester."

"Professor ter Horst, I really think you have to accept Cox's position on—"

Backer shifted uneasily.

"You got ants?" Kobol hissed at him.

"Ain't my turf. Better split. I feel like a sideshow geek."

A big black hand held him. "Man, you *are* the sideshow. Haven't you got that figured yet?"

Backer's reply was cut short by the bell and the scuffling of students. When, after a few curious glances, the classroom cleared, the tall old man lounged against the desk, waiting.

"Well? Finally come back to really get a decent education, Leon?"

Backer shook his head. "Just not my scene." He tried to leave, but again felt Kobol's strong grip.

"Is your friend Spartacus uncomfortable outside the arena, Leon?"

Backer stopped. "I'm not sure what that means, but I think I don't like it."

Kobol squeezed his shoulder even more tightly. "Prof, I wanted you to meet my new home boy. Backer's got some new problems and some old questions."

He added, in a ludicrous imitation of a whisper, "My man's on a short lease, Prof."

Ter Horst uncoiled his lanky frame and shambled toward Backer.

They stood there a moment, eye to eye, the professor and the biker.

"Why are you afraid of me?" asked ter Horst finally.

Thunder rattled the windows. An early September storm, Clint told himself, that was the only reason for his trembling.

"Why?" repeated the professor.

"It ain't you," Backer said, very low. "It's that dude in the Book. I'm afraid of getting suckered. I knew someone—" He stopped, caught his breath. "—bought a ticket out. But I figure . . . I figure there's lots of ways to eat your gun if *out* is what you want. I'm afraid that Book is just another way to get brain dead."

Ter Horst rasped, "You seem to possess adequate frontal lobes, Mr. Backer. I suggest you employ them, novel experience though it may be."

Kobol winced. "Professor, are you positive—"

"Not always, Mr. Kobol, but I'm usually correct. Why don't you leave us alone for a bit? Have a snack. The cafeteria food is as loathsome as you recall. Reassure yourself as to the integrity of your memory."

"And come back when?"

"Don't. Go home."

"I rode with him!"

"Hitchhike. Use your winning smile. That gold incisor is particularly captivating. Or go juggle your eyeball."

After Kobol's departure, ter Horst's gray head swiveled back to the trembling rider. "So state your objections. Use your reason."

"God is not a reasonable dude . . . If He is at all."

"I," said the professor, "am a reasonable being. Therefore I could not serve a Creator who was otherwise. Logically, I am limited in my reasoning and He is not. But to imagine Him as other than logical would be . . . unreasonable."

More thunder and September lightning snaked across the sky. Clint, still traumatized, felt himself shake again and cursed himself for it.

Their eyes, man, look at their eyes.

He forced himself to look up as the past danced before him. Through the mists he could discern ter Horst's rugged features.

Clint knew something: the Dutchman was not afraid.

Backer braced himself against a desk. "But why should there be a God? Who's to say all this didn't just . . . happen?"

"Something out of nothing?"

"Huh?"

"Think about it."

After a moment Backer blinked. "I get it. You mean . . . if something *is* . . . namely *us*, then something must've always been. But that don't make it your kindly Mister Jesus. Coulda been . . . an accident . . . The universe belched or something."

Ter Horst's jaw dropped. He stared past Backer at the rain-streaked window. "A UFO," he said, "on my campus!"

"What—?" Backer turned, and as he did ter Horst heaved himself to his desk, picked up a papier-mâché globe, and threw it—not gently—at the rider.

Backer's hand deflected it just in time. It splattered against his knuckles, the fragments littering the floor.

He lunged for ter Horst, who put the desk between them. "Crazy old German! Why—?"

"Dutch. And I didn't. A tremendous mass of paint and newspaper and glue just flew in over the transom, molded itself into a globe, and spun into your face—probably picking the spot it could damage least."

Backer crawled on top of the desk, arms extended. "You are nuts. Nothing just *happens* like that. You had to *make* it . . . Oh." His knee slipped, sending a textbook onto the floor.

"Never mind." The professor grimaced. "It's only Jaspers. But you've grasped the point, haven't you? And if so, please get down off my desk. I may need it again sometime."

Backer slid from the desk and inched back to the door. "You're just too foxy, Dutch. I gotta . . . I gotta think."

"Rider . . ." ter Horst's voice whipped out. "You're hurting."

"Everybody hurts." His hand was on the knob, but it wouldn't stay put.

"Everybody's got their maximum. Obviously you've reached yours. You want to roll the dice again, go on to death or madness? From the look of you, you've had enough of both."

Backer shut his eyes.

"Is that what you want? To go the way you've seen others go? Sometimes we have to be bent to our knees before we find a way onto our feet. He's here. He loves you. Let Him stand you on your feet."

"It's too late!" Too much loss of sleep, loss of blood, loss of Colt . . . Backer swayed.

"You're not dead yet. It's not too late."

Colt . . . I promised I'd take care of you, kid.

"I can't!"

"You can."

Thunder rattled the windows.

The old man sniffed. "You could also take a bath."

Backer lashed out, his knuckles rocking ter Horst's head back on its thick neck. The older man staggered.

"Outcast . . ." Ter Horst ignored the blood trickling from his lip. "He loved them even when in their fear and ignorance they did that to Him. And he loved *you* even then . . . as I do now, through Him. Come home, boy. It's your time."

He put both thick hands on Backer's shoulders, and it was a good thing, because the rider was slipping, falling down the wall, and the old man steadied him as he sank.

Backer dug his palms against his swollen eyes, and a sound he did not recognize, did not remember, rose in gasps from his chest.

Finally he wiped away the wetness with his sleeve and, looking up, said, "Show me . . . Show me how."

Backer spent the rest of the day with ter Horst. In the evening, over coffee in a corner shop, the professor finished his explanations. Backer finished making up his mind.

At his drawing board that night, Kobol heard the Harley's growl through the slap of the rain.

He shut off the small pool of light and padded to the front door. "You're mighty late, wonderboy," he began, then stopped.

Backer stood on the threshold, water dripping off his face and down the leather jacket. The two men stared at each other for a moment before Kobol silently moved aside.

Backer stepped in and walked across the carpet, leaving wet footprints in his wake.

"You okay, man?" Kobol spoke to the rider's back.

"I made it," Clint said at last, turning. Though he was just as battered, blood-splattered, and dirty, he was clearly changed.

Kobol laughed, and it was louder than the sudden peal of thunder. His big arms went crushingly around the rider.

"Daddy, you're gonna wake Luke." Jeremy, in blue sleepers, spoke sleepily from the doorway.

Deep laughter bounced again through the house.

"Let him wake, son," Kobol said, lifting his boy. "There are some sounds a man ought to hear."

———

Backer had come to Kobol's cabin intending to spend the night. He spent nine weeks. He chopped wood, repaired the roof, talked with Kobol and ter Horst, walked with Jeremy and Luke, and read. He even tried his hand at cooking.

"Anthracite for breakfast?" Kobol poked a fork at the two black lumps Clint plopped on his plate.

"They're eggs."

"Sin to jive so early in the A.M.," commented Kobol, whacking a lump with a knife.

"You ain't at your best in the morning, and me neither. Shut up and eat."

"Simultaneously?"

"Eat or stay hungry." Backer attacked his own portion.

"As Jeremiah said—"

"He didn't ever."

"But you don't even know what I'm about to—"

"Morning, Daddy 'n Clint." Luke trudged into the kitchen, his brother following.

"What's zis black stuff?" Jeremy peered sleepily into his plate.

"It's the subject of debate." Kobol rested his elbows on the table.

"I'd druther have some food."

"You guys don't appear exactly robust," their father said. "What time you get to bed last night? I know you were stacking up the z's when I came in from night class, but that was later than late."

"What's 'robust' mean?" Jeremy inquired.

"What you guys ain't," answered Backer, scraping the plates into the sink and replacing them on the table with a jug of milk and a carton of cornflakes.

"We hadda stay up late so Clint could finish his story."

"This is breakfast, not 'Boulder A.M.'" Backer shoved an empty bowl at Luke. "People always talk too much in the morning and at funerals."

"What's Clint saying, Daddy?" Jeremy aimed the box at his bowl and sprayed cornflakes all over the table.

"He's just what you call naturally morbid," said Kobol, flicking flakes from his lap.

"What's 'morbid'?"

"Later. What's this song and dance about hanging 'round to the smallies for a story?"

Backer shoved milk at the boy. "Eat, kid."

"He told us 'bout . . . 'bout 'Snow White and the Seven Bikers,'" Jeremy said.

"See," Luke explained, "there was these seven guys and they were little, like us—"

"Except they had tattoos all up and down—"

"And they wore black leather jackets with 'Munchkin' on the back—"

"Clinton, what on God's green globe you been telling these—"

"—And they hadda fight these bad guys, called the Little Red Riding Hoods—"

"And one of the dwarfs, Dorkie, got on his Harley—"

"This," said Kobol, "is grim indeed, but it does not come from the brothers of that name, nor is that the way things went."

"Things go the way you push 'em." Backer bent over his cereal.

"You have so much to learn in the time you got left," sighed Kobol.

"Next time," Jeremy said between bites, "Clint's gonna tell us all about 'Goldilocks and the Three Smokies.'"

"Historical revisionist." Kobol put his head in his hands.

———

The season turned, and Kobol spoke to Backer about a place in Denver, a coffeehouse, a way station for urban pilgrims.

"But if I tell Niklhas you're coming," Kobol said one autumn afternoon, "you'd better back up your word. He likes people to do like they say."

"A hardnose, huh?"

"Niklhas," Kobol said after a moment's reflection, "is a cat in a tree all by himself."

One morning in late October Backer awoke and felt the crispness of winter hanging in the air.

It was time.

"He didn't even say good-bye," Jeremy said that afternoon, staring out the window at the bare spot where the steel-and-black Harley had stood.

Kobol was silent for a moment, watching the leaves drift into the yard. Then he said, "You guys remember ol' Growley?"

"The big dog we used to have before Intrusion. I remember." Luke nodded. "What happened to him, Daddy?"

Kobol continued to stare out the window. "He was more wolf than dog. And he wasn't the kind to let things just happen to him. He made 'em happen."

He looked away from the window, then sank down on the sofa, his sons beside him. "One spring day there he was, a mongrel pup with his ribs stickin' out, standing by the kitchen door. Then 'long about December we found his big ol' pawprints in the snow, headed back toward the hills."

Luke grabbed the white hound about the neck. "Intrusion will never go away."

"Someday we'll look up and see that Intrusion's lived his whole doggy life, and then it'll be time for him to go on."

"You mean when he dies," Luke said. "That won't be until a long, long time."

"Seems like it now." The man ruffled his son's curly hair. "But it'll happen." His voice lowered. "Or maybe *we'll* go home first, and he'll have to say good-bye to us."

"Then we can't keep anything forever!" wailed Luke.

Kobol pulled his sons onto his lap. "This ain't a keeping world. But be thankful for the time the Lord lets someone walk alongside us in it. Like ol' Growley—"

"Or like Intrusion!"

"Or like a son." The man looked at his boys. ". . . Or like a friend." He glanced over his shoulder to the window, and to the bare spot beyond, already being covered by the drifting leaves.

"Don't Jesus let us keep *anything* forever?" Jeremy asked, his face buried in his dog's white mane.

Kobol was silent a moment, staring out the window. "He lets us keep Himself."

THE CITY

*T*he setting sun reflected off the gold-domed Colorado capitol building as Backer drove into Denver. As he rolled down East Colfax, the evening shadows stretched across the pavement ahead of his wheels.

Turn-of-the-century residences transformed into crumbling apartment warrens rubbed slumped shoulders against bars, tiny movie houses, liquor stores, coffee-houses.

Between a used magazine store and a porno movie theater stood the FishHouse, a converted espresso-house left over from the fifties, its glass door closed against the chill evening, a small hand-painted green *Icthus* fish swinging on hinges above it.

Hunched against the wind in his doorway, the magazine-shop proprietor flipped a cigarette butt into the gutter as a big blonde strutted by, thinly attired for the early Rocky Mountain autumn.

She nodded at the bookseller. "No business for you either, huh, Kelley? What this street needs is new blood."

The sound of the Harley brought their heads up into the wind.

"Just what this street needs, Nora," the man said. "Bike bandits."

Backer glided to the curb, switched off his machine, and stared for a moment at the light glowing inside the FishHouse. It took him a long moment before he shoved his keys into his jeans and swung off the seat.

The girl stood in front of him. "I love motorsickles," she said.

"Me too." He pulled off his gloves and slapped them absently against his sleeve, eyeing the swinging fish-shaped sign. Then he resolutely started forward.

Mistaking his direction, the girl moved in front of him again. "Great big man like you don't need to get his jollies in a movie fulla old men."

Backer's intense stare broke. He looked down at the girl, nodded. "I'm going *there*." He flicked a nod at the coffeehouse.

She looked at his bike, at his rumpled denims and seamed face. "Not neither."

"Am so too. Watch me." Gently he moved the girl aside.

A croaking chuckle followed him. He turned sharply in the FishHouse doorway. "What's funny?" he asked the smiling bookseller.

The man shook his head. "Nothing. Not anything. Never." His head disappeared inside his shop, and the door slammed.

Sighing, Backer squared his shoulders and jerked open the coffeehouse door. Light sprayed out over the threshold. He squinted, barely making out the scattered tables, swinging lamps, a few moving shapes, and the silhouette of a large man seated at a small round table, bent over a book.

Eyes glimmered in that large silhouette. "Shut the door from one side or the other please."

Backer swung his arm, and the glass rattled shut. "I'm Backer."

The silhouette unwound from the table and moved into the light. "Vince Niklhas."

"Yeah."

Kobol was large, but this man was a monolith. Golden hair swept downward from a wide brow, past cheekbones that might have been molded by Rodin. Ice-blue eyes cut through Backer as the big jaw opened and Niklhas announced, through perfect teeth, "I'm in charge."

"I'll just bet you are."

"Kobol told me you were coming. He and I did a tour of the Nam together."

"Hurrah for the sodjer-boys."

"And ter Horst vouches for you," acknowledged Niklhas, ignoring the sarcasm. His long arm reached a chipped mug beneath the tap of a tremendous coffee urn and handed the steaming cup to Backer.

Clint tilted the cup, scalded his tongue, but bit back the yelp. "I get just the tiniest feeling that you are less than thrilled."

"You're a Smart Guy. In the jungle Smart Guys got us killed."

"Heard the news? 'There's light at the end of the tunnel.'" He swung an arm out over the softly-lit interior. "And you got asphalt growing around you, not Asian swamp."

Niklhas smiled. "Would you be trying to tell me this isn't a jungle?"

Backer started a reply, but cut it short.

"It's jungle war, biker-man." Niklhas swallowed the steaming brew. "You should be knowing that."

"And Kobol should've given you a bulletin: you're not getting a plaster saint for the end table."

"Got no place to put a plaster saint." Niklhas poured more coffee for himself. "Doesn't fit the decor." He paused to sip. "Kobol said you were a sinner. This does not make you a candidate for the Twilight Zone."

"Thanks." Backer hadn't moved a step further in.

"I used to be a cop," Niklhas said.

"Swell."

"One time I had some trouble . . ." He tucked himself into his chair again. "And sit down, won't you please."

Backer hesitated, then drew out the chair opposite, under the lamplight.

"Wouldn't take a certain rake-off. Some guys followed me home. There was shooting. My wife was killed. I took one in the hand and one in the hip. I'm still on disability. It was a long time after the funeral before I stopped hating. When I did, I ended up here." He put down his mug. "But I still don't much like Smart Guys . . . or bikers."

Backer set down his own cup, sloshing the table. "I still don't like cops," he said.

They looked at each other. Niklhas lifted a hand. Backer took it.

They held the grip a little too long, blue eyes staring into red-flecked brown.

"We should get along fine," Niklhas said through his rows of perfect teeth.

"Jolly," Backer replied, massaging his crushed fingers below the table's edge.

The uneasy alliance between the two men grew into

respect and then friendship. Over the winter Backer was assimilated into the coffeehouse fellowship.

"We've been fished out of the dark," Niklhas told him. "And now we go fishing for others. We're fishers . . . every one of us."

Backer came to know and like the entire band: little Chavez, ex-junkie, ex-knife artist, with hoarse voice and ice-cube eyes; Joanie, child of the streets; Rob, ex-choir boy, ex-Satanist; and Dawn, copper-haired and violet-eyed, once a promising young painter, now blind from an auto accident.

Each came from a world alien to Clint, and in each he saw something of himself. He lived and studied among them through the winter evenings in the amber-lit coffeehouse.

At first he paid his way with repairs to the crumbling building, then with the salary from a mechanic's job at a Broadway garage. The slender remains of his paychecks went for supplies: lexicons, concordances, study aids. Commuting between Denver and Boulder, he was the pupil of three masters. With Niklhas, an ordained minister, he studied the Bible; with ter Horst he delved into philosophy; and in a Boulder gym he pumped iron with Kobol.

Gradually extra flesh and the marks of dissipation and stress melted away. Street people came to know him. He handled food giveaways with Dawn, arranged shelter for the homeless with Nik, talked to the gangs with Chavez.

And in the winter evenings, in the lamplight, he listened to Chavez strum his guitar and had long conversations with Dawn.

Then one frigid night before Christmas Backer and Chavez were trudging back toward the FishHouse from the homeless shelter.

"Got a match?"

Backer looked past his upturned jacket collar. Three boys in their teens stood huddled in the alley. One wore a navy-blue stocking cap. The others were bareheaded, and not one had a coat.

"We don't smoke anymore," Chavez said. "But I know a place you can get on the outside of a hot cup of coffee . . . and into friendly conversation."

"And I know where you can get—" The boy in the cap spat.

Backer stiffened, moving into the alley.

Chavez's fingers squeezed his shoulder.

"They ain't ready to listen." The two turned away, into the biting wind. Curses followed them.

"Maybe we should've helped them listen," Backer said through thin lips.

"You mean smash they skinny heads against the wall and tell 'em to accept Jesus or we'll pull they honky heads clean off?"

Backer half-laughed. "Maybe something along those lines."

"I like you, Backer. You're a good example."

"*Me?*"

"Every time I rap with you, I realize that God can save *anybody*."

Backer's reply was cut short by a scream from behind them. The two men ran back through the snow.

At the rear of the narrow alley, behind a rusted dumpster, the three boys were clustered around an aged derelict. Red flames flickered over them from a trash can against the wall.

"C'mon, man, you can't have *all* the heat," said the tallest boy, lifting the old man by his tattered lapels.

"This y'ere's my spot. You git one yo own!" The old man pushed at the boy. A bottle dropped from his pocket, and the alley filled with the smell of cheap whiskey.

Backer reached them first. "Let him go." He yanked the tall boy's arm, spinning him.

"Take all the heat then!" The second boy kicked at the can, sending burning trash and embers spraying through the cold night air.

The tallest boy threw the bum down into the flames. The old man shrieked and rolled, swatting at the cinders smoldering into his damp coat.

Backer shoved the tall boy aside as the second snatched up the half-full whiskey bottle and brought it down across the rider's ear. Blood and alcohol spilled over his face.

Still holding the jagged bottle neck, the second boy lunged at Chavez. The little man ducked and drove his shoulder into the boy, sending him flying.

"Rick, it's on me! It's on me!" the youngest one screamed as flaming debris sank sizzling into his cap and ragged shirt.

The old man clattered away up the alley.

"Get outta here!" the tall boy yelled.

"What about Darcey?" The second one hesitated.

"Go!" The tall one fled, the second on his heels.

Backer reached for the rolling, burning boy, who struggled blindly. He sent his fist down through the scarlet nimbus about the boy's head and felt the searing heat as his knuckles jarred against flesh. The boy went limp, and Backer pushed/dragged him into the snow piled up against the dumpster.

He kept shoving the boy further into the melting snow until suddenly the pain in his arm flared into a blue-white heat that exploded over his face and hair. Then there was a weight beating against his skin, flapping over him again and again.

Chavez had pulled his coat through the snow and was frantically slamming it over Backer, where the whiskey burned away at him.

A siren.

Muffled voices.

"Meat wagon!"

"Ju see his *face*?"

A low metal ceiling. Chavez staring down at him.

"Bet you could've talked 'em out of it," Backer mumbled as the ambulance rocked. "I always move too quick and think too slow. Sorry, m' man." He raised a hand to touch the swelling cut over Chavez's right eye.

But it wasn't his hand that reached up toward the little man's face. It was a red-black club, and when Clint saw it he instinctively snapped it back. It slapped into his face, and there was pain/pain/pain and he realized the truth.

8

THE HOSPITAL

"Not as bad as it might be," said the young doctor, his delicate fingers dancing over Backer's face. "When your hair grows out, it'll hide the scalp damage. As for your face—"

Backer used his good left hand to trace the crescent furrow that began below his right ear, sliced around his jaw, and burrowed up his right cheek, pulling the skin into a permanently sardonic grin.

"Grafts aren't completely out of the question, but—"

"My drug allergies. Yeah, you told me. And the expense."

"Yes . . . When that beard you're cultivating grows out, all the bandages come off, and as the tissue heals, well—"

"I'll be just James Dandy," Backer growled. "Whole new career possibilities in werewolf movies."

"And you'll recover most of the use of your right hand."

I'll recover *all* the use of my right hand." As if to prove the point, he held it up, bandages covering the ruin of the Wolves tattoo.

The doctor made appropriate responses, then departed.

Backer waited until the *flap flap* of the doctor's coat receded, then glanced over at Chavez. "Shoulda let you handle it. You could've done it. I still *believe*, but I'm just not cut out to be Crusader Rabbit."

"Breaking my heart." Chavez yawned. "Only guy ever made an expensive mistake. You heard Ben Casey. When your hair and beard grow out—"

"I'll look like a hairy well-done steak."

Chavez swung his short legs under his chair. "Sorry, *vato*, but you never were no Elvis. Beauty's only skin-deep, and you never did make it even that far."

A well-thrown pillow smacked the wall over his shoulder, and Chavez departed, wishing Backer a polite good afternoon.

The dull hospital days and nights were marked only by the light outside his window and the nurses' change of shifts.

Rob, the ex-Satanist came to see him; as did Joanie and even Kelley and Nora, the big blonde who worked the street. She had choice words for the alley-punks, but Clint shook his head, until the burning pain stopped the movement.

"No . . . I was on their turf. It was up to me to help."

"I don't see no *S* in a triangle on your chest, lover."

His bandaged paw held up the small cross that now dangled from his neck. "But I wear my sign."

In disgust Nora left. Not even Kelley could convince her of his cause.

When Dawn came, her violet sightless eyes filled as if they saw. Her fingers reached up to trace the outline of the bandages, but Backer stopped her with his good hand.

"Don't."

"Okay."

"I'm bored. Play a game with me?"

She tried to smile. "I'm not much good at Ping-Pong, and chess isn't my thing."

"Let's pretend. I'll pretend you don't have a good idea of what I must look like, and you pretend I look just like Niklhas really does."

"Oh, but I've touched Nik's face. I know he's . . ."

"Cuter than Mary Poppins. Yeah, and I bet you've got a good mental fix on my new, improved fabulous face."

"Clint, I—I see what you look like on the *inside.*"

"Ahh, you've been peeking. Shame."

If he was trying to make her uncomfortable, he was failing. "Clint, when—when I could see, I filled my place with beautiful idols."

"Why do chicks always feel they gotta confess to ugly men?"

"No, listen—Nature was my god, and painters, men like Turner and Constable, were my priests."

"The Impressionists. Yeah, I remember what we talked about before. I thought you were talking about guys who do Cagney and Jimmy Stewart on 'The Ed Sullivan Show.'"

She laughed. "You do remember. Men and women who found a new way to *see.* Not to paint the scene, but to put the light itself, or its reflection, on the canvas." She paused, remembering. "They were so beautiful. I'd read Whitman and Thoreau and look at a print of a Turner and feel like I was watching Prometheus."

"He's the guy who does Cagney?"

"You can't mix me up," she insisted. "I'm not going

to allow you to. In the myths Prometheus took fire from the gods and gave it to the human race."

"Does he still deliver? We could send out for dinner."

Now she sounded genuinely annoyed. "I'm trying to *tell* you something, and you keep hiding. I've never told anyone else . . ."

"Sorry, babe."

Squeezing his good hand, she said, "They were so beautiful . . . I still remember."

"Tough break."

"No." She released his hand. "That's what I'm trying to say. It wasn't tough . . . Not really . . . Not forever."

"So, like you're telling me blind is nice and burnt is beautiful?" The harsh words grated

"My whole life was spent . . . trying to catch the light, the beauty *outside* me. Once my . . . idols were gone, I had to reach down deep inside and find the Light."

"So God took your peepers and my hide just so we could enjoy the view?"

"Self-pity." She shook her head. "I know the flavor. It's a very addicting drug. Before I went blind, I was so hungry for Light I tried everything that was offered—acid, Mescaline. I tried to make the Light come when I called."

His face was hurting. "And you traded your sight for a metaphysical flashlight." He turned away.

"We were on our way to a dance when we were broadsided," she said. "Doug—my fiancé—was killed outright."

"You never said . . ."

"Not to the FishHouse—except Nik knows. Professor ter Horst sent me to him."

"The flying Dutchman gets around."

"I went through my painkillers, baseballed the

street stuff, but ter Horst told me it was self-pity I was hooked on."

Footsteps in the hall. Nurse time.

She spoke quickly. "When I finally found that Light—really there, for me—I finally got full. I knew it was all right for me . . . Even though my parents were of a different faith and wouldn't have me anymore. But Doug—he had it too, so I could let him go . . . Because I'll get him back."

"I hope you do, kid," Clint said to the departing clack of her heels. "Angels must have a lot in common."

In that bitter season of self-doubt, the events in the alley unreeled again and again in his mind. What could he/should he have done? Was this the price of Christianity? . . . Or just stupidity? Either way, he'd bear the marks for the rest of his life.

At night he lay in the bed, bandaged hand against his chest, eyes searching the ceiling shadows.

Is this how You protect Your own, Lord?

One clear afternoon, footsteps that could only come from Niklhas's size thirteens rang through the halls.

The big man leaned across the back of a chair.

"When my wife was killed, in the trailer—"

"I remember."

"She'd only been in this country six months. I brought her back from Nam. She . . . became a Christian because of me. I . . . was new . . . I told her He'd take care of us. When the shooting started, she crouched down behind the washer. Bullet went right through it. She . . . only lived three days."

Backer looked across the bed at him. "Why?" he asked simply.

Niklhas drew his lips back from perfect teeth. "Why did God allow—? I'm still working on it."

"Let me know what you discover, Augustine," Backer mumbled.

A voice like gravel crunching underfoot grumbled over Niklhas's shoulder.

"'All things work to the good for them that love the Lord.'" Ter Horst stumped into the room.

"Pull up a couple of chairs, Prof, and tell me what's good about this—" Backer stuck out his pale, freshly unbandaged fist. "Or this—" The fist struck the fissure in his face.

"Could be useful in frightening small annoying children." Ter Horst's large fundament flopped on the bed next to Backer's thigh. "But then, He never said everything would be rosy—He just promised to turn the worst into something best."

"That's it?"

Ter Horst sighed. "And perhaps . . . more . . . But you have to seek to find."

Backer looked away. A *thump* on the bed brought his head back around. "And regarding seeking, I brought this for you. Shall I secrete it beneath the covers so we can practice hiding and seeking?"

Picking up the hefty paperbound volume, Backer's red-flecked eyes opened wide. "G.E.D.?"

"You've exploited my verbosity long enough. Employ your current abundant leisure time in study. Take the high school equivalency exam. When next I hear your lumbering bootsteps on campus, let them be on their way to class."

Backer opened his twisted mouth to speak. Nothing came out.

"And don't be tardy," added ter Horst, brushing his rumpled suit and striding out the door. "I allow no one in class after my lecture has commenced."

"But I can't—I'm too old—"

"Cluck," Niklhas said. "Cluck. Here . . . this is from Kobol." He dipped a hand into his pocket and withdrew a red rubber ball. It bounced onto the bed. "He said it once struck your fancy."

Pulling his eyes from the book, Backer stammered, "Struck my face, which is not so fancy. But—"

Niklhas gripped Backer's weak right wrist, then plunked the ball between his fingers. "You can work your weak hand while you work your weak mind."

Backer's eyes darted from the ball in one hand to the book in the other."

Snapping a finger against the ball, Niklhas said, "Personally my money's on the ball."

"Yeah?"

"Prove me wrong." Niklhas stopped at the door. "By the way the FishHouse got a new resident yesterday. A Diversion from the court. I pulled old strings."

Unconsciously Backer began to squeeze the ball in his right fist while he stared at the book in his left. "Uh huh."

"Name's Darcey," Niklhas said casually. "The kid from the alley."

The ball bounced to the floor. "The kid who gave me . . . this?"

Without turning Niklhas asked, "We'd been talking about . . . when I . . . lost my wife?"

"Yeah?"

"It was a biker that did it." Kneeling, Niklhas scooped up the ball in his right hand, the one with the puckered bullet-scar below the knuckles.

"See you back home." He tossed the ball back onto the bed.

THE STREETS

"Today?"

"Everything off." The resident sent his scissors slicing through Clint's gauze. First the face, then the hand.

Looking down, he saw a thin, pale right hand and a purplish smear where the Wolves mark had been.

One by one he curled his fingers. It was still work, but they all bent.

"Nice healing," the resident said without enthusiasm. "Could've been much worse."

"Then how come you're not offering me a mirror? What's up, doc?"

Wordlessly the physician held out his hand. A nurse placed a small glass disk in his palm.

Backer reached out and forced his white fingers to wrap themselves around the resident's wrist.

"I'm nearsighted, doc. I'd wear glasses, but they're just not cool." He brought the mirror near his ruined face.

"Jesus." He didn't know himself if he meant it as a curse, a prayer, or an exclamation of recognition.

The beard was tawny, the hair long in the style of the times, and the crescent furrow reamed his face.

So the lopsided grin was permanent, but there was an expression in the eyes that hadn't been there before.

"Could've been much worse," the resident repeated, rising.

Backer tried to smile, and in the effort he suddenly recognized the familiarity of the face in the mirror.

There was suffering in the eyes—quiet, undefeated— as he flexed his wounded hand.

Maybe Christ looked like that, he thought before banishing the words as blasphemous.

But Dawn's violet eyes and her talk of grasping the Light from down inside stayed with him as March rain pelted the window and his attendants left him, staring at his own alien reflection.

———

Early March slush sprayed up against the windows as Chavez raced the fellowship's old bus back through the puddles to the coffeehouse.

"I just put in that gearbox couple months ago," Backer grumbled through his beard, fingers clenching the red rubber ball. "You can't grind 'em like a tortilla."

Nervously he continued to squeeze. Strength pulsed through the thickening digits. *FLEXflexFLEXflex.*

. . . *almost back to normal,* he thought. *Maybe stronger. Funny—*

Chavez chortled. "Don't tell me about tortillas, you *pachuko* with the meatball face. I didn't see you on the streets of East L.A."

"I been there. You just didn't look in the right zoot suit."

They were pulling to the curb.

"Zoot suits!" Chavez killed the engine. Backer could see the eager crowd of faces in the rain at curbside. "You're not only messed up, you're *old, mano*."

Clint saw Nora and Kelley push to the front of the crowd, saw the look on Kelley's face, quickly masked.

"Yeah," Clint said as the doors hissed open. "I get off here."

Inside, the entire FishHouse population packed the trembling building.

Most of them were already familiar with the twisted grin beneath the beard. But he saw how the look in his eyes sent their glances sliding away.

Except for Dawn. Her sightless eyes were leveled at him, then her arms were around him, and surely the murmur of welcome in his ear held more than simple kindness.

Jostling though the shoulder-slapping crowd, he gripped hands, slapped palms, hugged and was hugged again.

In the far corner, against the stairwell, there was a new face. Thin to gauntness, little more than a child, a small reddish-scar on the forehead, almost hidden by the hair that fell into the eyes—

The kid from the alley.

"This is Darcey," Niklhas said.

The boy held out his right hand.

FLEXflexFLEXflex went Backer's fingers.

After a long moment he flipped the ball into his left hand and slipped his right firmly into the boy's grip.

The kid began to stammer about That Night and how grateful he was—

Backer heard none of it. Staring at the eager young face, he furrowed his heavy brow, trying to erase the sudden image of Colt, almost as young, smiling desperately, the gun barrel lifting to his mouth . . .

But that was then and this was now.

Just focus your mind right down, he told himself. *This is just another kid, and we're like a crowd on a postcard, having a picnic.*

Scenery's here, wish you were beautiful.

Suddenly aware of the eyes on the two of them, Backer withdrew his hand.

"What can you do?" he asked the kid abruptly.

"D-do?" the boy stammered.

"I know your Daddy's rich and your mama's good-lookin'. But this is the FishHouse, kiddy, and around here we gotta work." He looked up as the ceiling creaked ominously. "Sometimes we just gotta keep the roof from caving in."

Sadness passed over the boy's face. He dropped his hand.

"Daddy's rich, maybe Ma was good-lookin' in her day, but I can work."

"For sure?"

The determined look reminded him again of Colt.

"You try me."

"I will. I surely will."

━━━━━━

As the Colorado spring began to assert itself, Backer slipped into now-familiar paths. To his amazement he discovered what a thin margin of difference his looks made to the people on the streets. But he was marked as unique. He was a fixture, like the pioneer statue-fountain at the intersection of Broadway and Colfax.

Hookers knew him. They knew that he was neither a trick to be turned, nor a judge to defy. Nora, the six-foot blonde, defended him passionately.

"Join us," Backer urged.

"Eddie would kill me."

"I know Eddie," answered Backer grimly. "I'll have a talk with him."

"Eddie don't let no one leave his stable."

"Do you want to?"

"I didn't used to." She looked away. "But now . . . yeah, yeah, maybe."

"You know whose side I'm on."

"I know."

"Do you want in?"

"Yeah." She stared. "Maybe."

He didn't push.

He talked to Eddie.

Eddie took a Greyhound for the coast.

Nora moved into the FishHouse.

The gangs began to trust him.

A delegation came, asking for "Captain Blood . . . y' know, that buff dude with, like, that pirate grin" to mediate between warring factions.

"Captain Blood, huh?" Niklhas asked as the boys swaggered off.

"Could be worse." Backer shrugged, wondering where he'd heard that name before. The memory slipped away.

But he went to the gangs, stood on the disputed turf,

spoke quietly, and there was no rumble at West High that weekend.

"Yeah, I heard 'em talk about Captain Blood," Chavez remarked. "But I think they oughta call you Igor . . . Or maybe Quasimodo, y' know?"

The ripped yellow vinyl couch on which he reclined flipped over—with him on it.

One evening as the scent of lilacs drifted in from the small patch of earth allowed by the ubiquitous pavement, Dawn approached him.

"I want to touch your face," she said, raising her fingers.

Backer jerked his head away.

"New career for me," she explained. "I can't see, so I can't paint. But my fingers aren't blind. I bought some clay—I'm going to try modeling. Think I'll try to do a bust of the Apostle Peter."

"You can do it," Backer said.

"But I need a model—someone whose face I can touch, who'll sit for me."

"Niklhas, of course. He was born for it."

She laughed. "For Michelangelo, maybe. I see—pardon the expression—Peter as an ordinary guy, plain but strong. It was his heart that was outsize, after God touched it. That's what I want to show."

Her fingers began to delicately trace Backer's features. Backer stopped her. "I'm . . . burned."

"I can ignore it if you can." So the first of a series of evenings began, the rider and the girl talking, she struggling to master the new medium.

After each session Dawn threw a cloth over her work.

"When will you let me see it?" he asked.

"When I know I can do it."

———

A Saturday workout with Kobol in late spring was disrupted when the rumpled figure of ter Horst strolled into the Boulder gym.

Kobol leaned against the wall and wiped sweat from his face.

"An honor, Herr Professor. I've just been initiating our impetuous pupil into the first stages of kung fu."

He held out a hand and helped Backer to his feet.

"Both Leon and Nik," the rider panted, "go on about it. One of those in-the-Nam numbers. Figured I'd find out how good a middle-aged draftsman could be."

He squatted on the mat. "I found out."

"'Bodily exercise,'" observed ter Horst, "'profiteth little.'"

Backer shook his head. "Out of context, and in your case entirely hypothetical."

Tugging the soaking T-shirt up over his head, Backer unconsciously displayed the new muscle that rippled beneath his scars.

"At least I've expanded your vocabulary beyond 'vroom vroom.'"

A booklet flipped out from ter Horst's gnarled hand, and Backer's fingers sliced through the air to catch it.

"Impressive," grumbled the professor. "Pity your mental grasp has not grown equally catlike. However, little of the text you now hold contains words of more than two syllables, so attempt to comprehend."

"I'll use both eyes." Backer snapped open the folder. "Summer session?"

Ter Horst inclined his head an eighth of an inch. "I have condescended to lead a very elementary class during the summer session. You, Neanderthal, should be able to matriculate by then."

"I'm still getting ready for the G.E.D."

"You," sniffed ter Horst, "are scared."

That evening, as Backer sat for Dawn and her deft fingers moved from his face to the clay and back again, Darcey stood in front of him and began a rapid-fire mumbling.

"Huh?" Backer shifted. The boy swallowed, then went on in a rush, his words crushed together.

"I was a senior before I dropped out. I dropped out because I got sick of my mom always trying to tell me what to—anyway, before I hit the streets I was ready to graduate, and I thought maybe . . . maybe I could make up to you for the way you look. I mean . . ."

Dawn giggled, then shook burnished-copper waves of hair from her face. "I'm sorry," she murmured as she saw the boy flush.

"I might, maybe, go home next month, and I thought before then I could help you pass your G.E.D."

Backer flexed the ball he still carried in his now-thick right fist. "Is it that obvious I'm scared?"

"I could help," repeated Darcey stubbornly.

In the subsequent evenings, the shaggy-brown brow of Backer and the straw-blond one of Darcey could be seen poring over notebooks, texts, and the battered G.E.D. volume.

"I'm going to be an electronics engineer," Darcey told him as they worked.

"When you get big, huh? What can you do with an engine?"

The boy displayed an uncanny knowledge of everything that hummed. Residents of the block began to complain about the line of vehicles blocking the alley behind the FishHouse. Backer handled the mechanical end, Darcey the electrical systems.

As the two were hiking back down 16th Street from a "house call" on a Rambler station wagon, Darcey poked a thumb at a towering white office building off to the right.

"Lemme show you something."

They took the outside elevator—in '70, one of the first in the area—up to the observation roof. Someday it would hold a restaurant, but now it was only a bare roof surrounded by chain-link fence. They leaned on the railing and stared across the city. The permanent smog-inversion layer had not yet emerged, and to the west the Rockies rose up forever.

"My dad had an office here. He's an engineer. After the divorce we'd come up here and talk. He still liked me then."

"You wanna pay a call on him?"

"Not there now. Workin' on an oil job in Saudi Arabia. But then it was fun to visit. He even got my brother a summer job as the midnight rent-a-cop up here."

"Let's go, Darce."

"Dad never found out that my brother used to let some of the guys in late at night. We'd fool around up here." He nodded downward. "We'd even take the outside elevator—y' know how easy it is to jump-start this little vertical box?"

Backer put his hand on the boy's arm.

"We'd do this . . ." Darcey shrugged loose, jumped to the top of the fence, and balanced against the wind blowing in from the Rockies.

"Stop acting like a stupid kid."

"But I am a stupid kid." The boy hopped down. "Look what I did to you . . . among others."

"It's over."

"Funny." Darcey leaned over the railing. "My brother gets killed in a jungle halfway around the world, my dad runs overseas, my mom wraps herself up in her glad-hand charities, and I find my natural level on the streets roasting old men and bikers."

"Shut up."

Darcey smiled. "On the bright side, we know that life is hard and then you die, huh, Clint?"

"Sometimes." Backer moved to the stairwell, remembering a night on a mountain. Then he faced the boy. "But sometimes a body can find something—Someone—better and stronger than death."

"Like you found, Captain Blood?"

Backer looked into the boy's eyes. "Like you found, Easy Money." They slid down the glass elevator shaft in silence, passing the floor where Darcey's father had once worked. All the way down, Darcey's blue eyes stared up at the window.

———

A week later Backer was returning wearily from his job at the Broadway garage when Niklhas pulled up to the curb in the old bus. The door swung open on the April evening.

"Bike break?"

"Such a warm night, I left my Harley at the garage. You lonely?"

Niklhas had interrupted Backer's musings on the future. The kid had helped him. The exam next week was as good as aced. With ter Horst's backing, he'd enter college in the summer; he had some money put away. He couldn't be mistaken about Dawn; she liked him—she could not see the ruin of his face . . . He could tell her . . .

"Darcey's mother came by today." Niklhas spoke from behind the wheel. "The heiress herself."

"Heiress, huh?" Backer climbed into the bus.

"You don't know? Anna Beaucage Alexander. Her grandfather Charles Beaucage found a silver mine up above Leadville and then came to Denver to play with his newspaper-scandal sheet. Anna B. spends her time building theaters, stocking art museums, and writing editorials for the paper. Still elevating the family name to match the family fortune."

"Must be somewhat annoying, having a kid on the streets." They were lurching into gear.

"Most annoying. I was there for the end of her visit. 'Ungrateful brat' was about the nicest part. She called him a common thief, and he shot back, 'I guess blood tells.' He stomped off just as a kid will do, and she's having him removed, to Juvy. Says he's still doing drugs."

"Juvy," scowled Backer. "Was there one time, down the road a piece. Doesn't matter which state—don't never hit the Hall if you can help it."

Niklhas's eyes sought Backer's in the rearview. "Is he using?"

"Stuff's easy to get. People have been known to screw up." He stared back into the mirror. "But I don't think Darcey has . . . yet."

The bus took a dangerous curve.

"He used to freebase," Backer added.

"Well, now we find him locked in the upstairs FishHouse bathroom, and he's not talking or walking."

Niklhas glanced over his shoulder. "He'll talk to you, I think."

"Why didn't you bust the door down?"

"Way to go, Doctor Spock. No, almost everybody's at the rally 'cross town tonight. I've just got Dawn there with him while I wile away my time searching the streets for bike bums."

"You think he'll do something stupid?"

Again Colt's face floated to the surface of his mind.

Death ain't no big thing.

Niklhas gunned the engine.

Lights were out at the storefront when the bus screeched up, except for a small glimmer from the upstairs bathroom window.

"Kid's still in there." Niklhas slammed a lever, opening the door of the bus.

Backer was already on the pavement, hand on the knob.

Then he paused and walked back to the bus.

"Let's play it this way—" he began.

That action saved him as the coffeehouse exploded, tossing him back against the big front wheel of the bus.

Niklhas was screaming, wrenching at the shattered coffeehouse door, his words lost in the many-tongued roar of flame erupting from every window and crack of the FishHouse.

"Move!" Backer threw himself into Niklhas, and the men fell backward as a smoking pile of wood and brick smashed to the pavement from above.

"Dawn . . ." Niklhas said through a split lip, struggling to get up.

Another explosion and the walls of the FishHouse bulged outward, groaned.

"Boiler must've blown!" Backer shouted.

Niklhas tugged again at the door. But the inside ceiling had collapsed, and debris blocked the entrance. Beyond the fallen timbers Backer could see the smoke-enshrouded banister already in flames.

"Fire escape . . ." Backer kicked through the trash cans in the narrow alleyway between the blazing coffeehouse and the adjacent magazine store. He ran to the rear of the building, then swung onto the old iron fire escape, Niklhas at his heels.

The two clattered up the rungs to the second-floor balcony.

With another rumble, an iron arm of the fire escape swung away from the disintegrating wall, tilted, and slammed back against the building. The men toppled into the alley.

Backer coughed smoke from his lungs, fighting to his feet. He saw Niklhas sprawled in the rubble, unmoving.

The narrow bathroom window shattered, and a small form pitched out headfirst, tendrils of fire coiling over it as it plummeted into a mound of trash.

Pulling the hysterical boy from the rubbish, Backer saw that his face was lacerated from half a dozen glass cuts. There was a wild look in his eye.

"No burns?" he asked, shaking the child.

"N-no."

"Where's Dawn?"

The blue eyes cleared. "Only me in there, Clint. I was gonna get high and then go where we . . . go someplace and finish it. Told Dawn to beat it or I'd O.D. right there. She left. House was dark. Sorry about—"

"Dawn doesn't use lights!"

A woman's scream. Upstairs, beyond the narrow broken bathroom window that was billowing with smoke.

"No," Darcey said, "I didn't mean—"

"Clint, help me! Help me—" Dawn shouted.

A timber crashed onto the pavement, smothering her cry.

Up and down the old building Backer stared, trying to find a way in.

The smell of smoke and the fire's hiss bit into his mind. He felt the scars on his face knot, then pull upward into a tangle of damaged nerves and muscle. He remembered the blue-white fireball that had traveled up his arm and eaten his face.

Dawn.

Help me, he mumbled. *Show me what to do.*

Pushing past the stammering boy, he skidded over the refuse and slammed through the rear door of the magazine shop.

Kelley was ramming down the phone. "Called the Fire Department!" he cried, turning toward the front of the building. "We gotta—"

A fist gripped his arm, twisted him halfway around.

"Stairs?" Backer shouted, sirens already wailing in the distance.

Kelley pointed, then ran for the door.

Backer took the old wooden steps three at a time, past the second-floor living quarters, up into the small attic.

Stacks of magazines slid aside as he pushed through to the small dormer window, kicked out the glass, gripped the sill, leaned out.

He stared down at the entire trembling structure of

the FishHouse. The bottom two floors looked like Hell's basement.

Flames were dancing on sections of the roof, but *there*—

A dormer window, like this one, a small swing-out pane beneath a peaked roof, at the near corner of the FishHouse. It opened on a musty attic where old lamps and desks were stored; things to be repaired if and when. Just yesterday Backer and Darcey had lugged an old Magnavox up there, shoving it under the eaves.

No fire there . . . yet.

Clint squeezed himself through the window opening, almost three stories up.

The FishHouse window was twelve feet away, straight across.

Fear hit him as his brain filled with the smell of his own charring flesh.

He jumped.

Fingers of his right hand jabbed through the glass as he slammed against the FishHouse wall. It was hot, but the extra strength in his marred hand held on.

He swung his left hand up, dug it into the glass splinters, and gripped.

But the weaker left hand could not hold, and he slid a foot down the building, over the flames. His right fingers jerked, then squeezed, and he dragged himself up into the narrow attic. Smoke clouded the small space, and he hit the floor, crawling below the fumes.

Reaching the staircase at last, he slithered down the steps and scrabbled to his feet at the rear end of the second-floor hallway. Walls on both sides were blazing.

Peering through the tunnel of flame, he saw Dawn at the far end, back against the wall, hands at her face.

He called her, and she cried out, stumbled forward, tripped against a splintered beam, and disappeared.

Firelight like flame on a candle surrounded him as he forced his way through the smoke.

He groped, finally found the girl's body, the cuffs of her bell-bottoms smoldering.

Slapping at the jeans, Backer heaved her to her feet. She wrapped her arms about him wildly. Together they stumbled through the hall, dodging flames and crashing timbers.

A hunk of ceiling hit the floor by the attic staircase door. The wooden door frame was gone in a minute.

Backer jerked away, guiding the girl toward the lower staircase. It wasn't there.

Yelping with pain as Backer tugged at her fingers, Clint dragged Dawn back into the tunnel of flame, aiming for the bathroom door.

A tower of flame shot up, taking the bathroom door and the entire side of the hallway with it.

There was a small bedroom to the right of the bathroom, and Backer kicked a boot into the blistering paint on the door. It swung open on a room dissolving into fire.

But there was a window at the far end, framed by burning drapes . . . and a small stretch of floor not yet engulfed.

He started forward with the girl. Dawn screamed as the floor dropped away beneath them.

She slid into the hole, dragging Backer after her.

As he dropped through the hole, his boot swung out, caught desperately at an iron bedstead. The already-burning bed slid several feet before it wedged tight against an old bookcase.

With the toe of his boot crammed into the corner of the bed-frame bars, his boot stopped his slide.

He was hanging head down by the toe of one boot,

dangling through the hole in the floor, desperately clinging to Dawn's elbows.

The girl screamed while she swayed with her feet just above the molten sea that had been the coffeehouse living room.

Ignoring her cries, Clint tried pulling up with his leg.

No good. The bed frame joggled and he slipped forward, almost losing the girl.

"Clint!"

His boot dug in, and inch by painful inch he pulled himself and the girl back into the upstairs bedroom.

Clint finally made it to his feet, dragging Dawn after him.

There was nothing left to the room.

But through the glare he caught a glimpse of the streetlight beyond the window.

Covering Dawn with his body as best he could, he rushed them both into the furnace—through the heat and to the glass rectangle of night, framed in flames.

Beneath them Backer saw the fire truck, its Denver County white body sliding to the curb.

To the left was the pile of trash into which Darcey had plummeted. The boy was gone, but Niklhas was there, gesturing to the firemen pouring from the truck.

Don't you ever stop giving orders? he wanted to shout as the ceiling began to spread apart and the old Magnavox fell through. It hit the floor beside them, exploded, toppled into the cavern of flames below.

The floor creaked, groaned, and began to yawn apart.

Clint kicked out the window glass, swung the girl up into his arms, brushed his lips across the top of her coppery hair, and flung her, with every ounce of strength in his arms and back, out the window, at the pile of trash.

10

THE TOWER

Backer watched Niklhas run at Dawn, arms out to break her descent. He saw them collide, the pair sinking into the debris.

He made certain they were both sufficiently away to his right before he jumped just as the roof caved in all around him.

He felt the extreme pains up his legs as he landed, but he rolled and made it to his feet. "Kung fu, God bless you."

He was in one piece.

He looked over and saw Dawn clinging to Niklhas.

"Can you," Nik asked over her trembling head, "find him?"

Backer knew where to find Darcey.

He ran through the darkening streets to the Broadway garage, kicked his bike into life, and gunned through evening traffic, down 16th Street, past the yellow cube of the May Company department store, past the Paramount Theater, then veering right and thudding into the curb beside the icy-white tower with the glassed-in outside elevator.

He raced inside to the elevator doors, hit the button. The doors slid open . . . Just like he figured. The kid still had it wired . . . just like he was. Or maybe it just hadn't been locked yet. If others were still up there, maybe the boy wouldn't—

But Darcey was alone on the roof when Backer stepped through the doorway, his skinny body tilted askew over the fence as he stared down at the blue-shadowed street.

The crunch of a boot on gravel sent Darcey up the fence. He balanced precariously on the railing.

Approaching slowly, Backer stuck his hands in his hip pockets.

"Air smells good up here, Darce. Got summertime in it."

The boy's haunted face stared down. "Got the scent of blood in it too . . . Did I kill Dawn?"

"She's only scared . . . and singed around the edges. Nothing a trip to the May Company jean department and a little sleep won't fix."

"Niklhas? I saw her hit him."

"He's a little ticked, I imagine. But you couldn't damage that golden hide with an arc welder . . . But you—you look uptight as a wound yo-yo . . . and just as stable."

Darcey teetered on the fence. "Top a' the world, Ma!' . . . as Jimmy Cagney once observed."

"I saw that flick. Since he said that and up and died, I got to figure there was a flaw in his reasoning."

Darcey turned away, looked out over the city. His long blond hair whipped into his face.

"I'm ticked myself, Darce." Backer edged closer.

The boy swallowed. "I imagine."

"But I'll get over it." Backer shrugged inside his jacket. He stepped up to the fence, put his arms across it.

"But if you go down there, achieve terminal squash, I don't think I will get over it." He glanced up at the wobbling boy beside him. "Matter of fact, I'll be somewhat annoyed with you from tip to tootsies."

"I almost wasted Dawn!" Darcey shouted, wobbling. "Almost blasted you too!"

"Wasted is bad," agreed Backer. "Like the Concerned Citizens say before they empty their ashtrays out car windows, 'Ecology now!'"

Silence.

"My brother Colt wasted himself, y' know."

"Huh?" The wind was rising, and Darcey's foot slipped. He wobbled, recovered his balance.

"He was so scared, scared of messing up, scared of dying, that he got to telling himself Death was nothing. So one fine night while he was standing on top of the world, Death came and dragged him down."

Backer gazed down at the city. "Wasted all to pieces . . . I saw the pieces."

Darcey swallowed.

"And all I can hope for Colt is that nothingness is the worst thing he found . . . after . . ."

Slowly, so very slowly, Backer's arm reached up to steady the boy's leg.

Immediately Darcey stiffened, ready to jump before he could be pulled away.

But Backer only stood there, his arm bracing the boy against the wind. "There was a Man once . . . For a long time I thought it was just a story, like Robin Hood. But it's true . . . He showed us that Death is true too, and it's hungry. He went up against Death's appetite, and He pulled its fangs."

Releasing the boy, the rider returned to the stairwell.

"I don't think Death is nothing. I think it's a black

Hungry inside your heart and mind, and it eats and keeps eating . . . always. Unless . . . unless you take Christ as the doorway out. He's the Something that can take you out of Nothing."

Darcey swayed on the fence. "I turned you into a grinning freak. I almost killed your artsy girlfriend. Your brother killed himself. How do you do it? How do you hold on to what you believe?"

For a long while there was only the sound of the wind and the rumble of traffic far below.

"I can't," Backer said at last. "He holds on to me."

Darcey began to sway, tilting out over the abyss. "How could He hold on to a screw-up like me?"

"Screw-ups are what He does best maybe." Backer shrugged. "Too late now for Colt." The words burned his throat as he said them. "But you still got the option." He swung open the stairwell door. "For another minute or two anyway."

"You're not gonna try and save me?"

"Kid, I can't save anybody." He stepped through the doorway, and his voice carried back. "But He'll take care of you."

"I—I want another chance. I want—"

Backer was there to catch him and take him to the ground.

Lifted in the biker's arms and carried to the stairwell, Darcey thought he heard someone whisper, "Another chance."

And Clint's answering growl, "This time."

But he was fainting, and was never sure afterward what he had heard.

THE CAMPUS

*I*n the warm morning air Backer and Niklhas stood at the curb, surveying the remains of the FishHouse and the rest of the burnt-out block.

"Could be worse," Niklhas said.

"How?" asked Backer, stepping aside as Chavez heaved another boxload of blackened debris into the street.

In the hours that followed, the FishHouse refugees salvaged what they could while Niklhas used up the phone lines and most of the favors due him, making temporary arrangements for members of the fellowship.

"We'll build it again," Backer said, kicking aside a book too blackened to be deciphered.

"We'll do better." Niklhas shook his perfectly-molded head. "But not here anymore, I think . . . And not just now . . . And not with you."

"What?"

"Exam tomorrow . . . You recall?"

"It'll be weird without Darcey to lead the cheering section. I got used to the little weasel."

But it was easier knowing that though Darcey was

back in Juvenile Hall, forces for his release had already been set in motion.

Niklhas still had a little juice. No one (miraculously?) had been injured, and there was a change in the boy, as obvious as it was sincere.

"The way he's acting will go a long way," Niklhas remarked. "And he turns eighteen this week. Now if only his old lady would back him a little . . ."

"If Momma's on Boardwalk," Backer asked, "what's Darcey doing on 'Go to Jail, do not pass Go'?" He finished strapping his gear aboard the Harley, swung on, and looked back at the FishHouse, perhaps for the last time.

Niklhas shrugged big shoulders. "Family flaps only their right wing, and when their oldest boy was flapped back from the Nam in a body bag the parents blamed each other. Dad split for Saudi. Mom grabbed onto Darcey, the house liberal, with both hands. Darcey flew the coop."

"Maybe we could talk to Anna Beaucage Alexander." Backer kicked the bike alive.

"An ex-cop and an ex-biker?"

"I'm still a biker."

Niklhas snorted. "I don't see it happening." He slapped the knapsack strapped to the back of the bike. "Go get ready to climb higher. God'll show us what to do for Darcey. Our best bet is the little bit of juice I have going with his Probation Officer. He's seen me pull some rabbits out of hats."

"And the FishHouse?" Backer called as he rolled forward.

"We've already seen a lot about resurrection." Niklhas grinned, showing his perfect teeth, as Backer twisted the gas and shot up Colfax.

———

He passed the G.E.D. The same day, in Kobol's cabin, he began preparing for a full class load. But the focus of his concentration was pierced by the jangle of the telephone.

"For you." Kobol flipped the receiver at him.

Panther-quick, Backer caught it. "Tell 'em," whispered Backer, a palm on the phone and his jagged nose in a book, "I've been raptured . . . or executed . . . Anything at all. Just let me study, will you please."

"Mercy mercy me," Kobol gasped, his gold tooth glinting in his wide-open jaw. "Not only would you have a good Christian man tell a story—and that's not even taking in the obvious fact that you're asking subterfuge of the most perfect physical specimen God ever created—but you'd have me give a story to Anna B. Alexander herself."

Still muffling the receiver, Backer's heavy brow went up as he asked, "The newsprint queen herself?"

Kobol sniffed. "Rocky Mountain Richlady comes to dinner. Shall I save her a place at the head of the table?"

Mrs. Alexander's words were terse: her son Darcey had turned eighteen; her son Darcey was somehow changed; her son Darcey wanted to enroll at C.U.

Backer's lips moved. "Can he—but he's—"

"You don't have a handle on this, do you, Mister Backer? It's not who my son is or isn't—it's who I am. If I say yes, his probation officer will say yes. If I call some friends, the school board will clear it. His SATs—before he went bad—were in the highest 2 percent."

"Then send him, lady!"

"I will not be made to play the fool again. Darcey has dragged our name through the dirt . . . The Beaucage name. During his rite of passage he's hurt a good many people . . . quality people."

There was a pause.

"Including you, Mrs. Alexander?"

"Including you, Mr. Backer. I understand you're disfigured."

"I wasn't too well 'figured' going out the gate. Darcey and I are . . . are friends."

"That . . . is what I don't understand. That is why I want to talk to you."

"My schedule's very full, Mrs. Alexander."

There was a deep chuckle. "Mine's fuller, I should think. But if I need a recommendation, ask Professor ter Horst."

"Ter Horst?" But he was holding a dead line.

———

Shambling across the blacktop behind the Administration Building, ter Horst commented, "When her eldest son died and her husband left, she went to pieces. But she does keep those pieces . . . in high profile." He nodded at Backer. "Very high on the board of her very High Church, I recall."

"So is she . . ." asked Backer. "A believer, I mean?"

Ter Horst sighed. "To judge from the conversations we had twenty years ago, when we were at school, she was . . . then. But answers are simple before you know the questions."

They cut by a well-used Volkswagen bug. A thick-legged girl was bent beneath its rear hood while a beefy young man in a letter jacket peered over her shoulder.

"It's *not* the solenoid, Gary." Her muffled voice carried over the upraised hood.

Something in the voice made Backer stiffen and stop.

"I bet you wouldn't know a solenoid if you were introduced to it formally." She popped her head up, shaking auburn bangs from her eyes.

"It's the solenoid," Letter Jacket repeated, arms folded. "That little thing there. And you can't get it replaced tonight. Better come back with me."

"This I've heard before." Then she saw ter Horst. "Professor! Do you know how to fix a bug?"

Ter Horst ran thick fingers through his hair. "Difficult as this concept will be for you to digest, dear Lynne, I do not actually know everything . . . Only a full two-thirds."

"Then I must assume," she laughed, "mechanics lie in the shadowy realm of the remaining third?"

"If, as you embark upon your final semester, you still have not grasped my maxim to never assume, then obviously I have not been a successful mentor."

"So it is . . . my final semester." Her smile wavered briefly. "But you're always successful as a mentor. You assured me of that."

"And I assure you that my large companion can no doubt successfully revive your vehicle with a speed Lazarus might find familiar." He shoved Backer toward the car.

The boy blocked his access. "It's the solenoid."

"Yeah . . . Excuse me." Backer dipped below the hood, fingers moving. In thirty seconds he straightened. "Try turning it over."

The VW started.

She stuck her head out the window. "A laying on of hands?"

"A reattachment of a distributor wire." His tone was strained enough for ter Horst—never one to avoid contemplation of a pretty face—to glance from the girl to the rider.

"You always keep trained monkeys with you, Prof," asked Letter Jacket, "to impress young girls?"

"Sometimes brings along his organ grinder." Backer slammed the hood.

"Maybe he should take solenoids." The girl giggled.

"Incidentally, that was the carburetor you were pointing at."

"Funny, funny man." The boy glowered. "Are you the new parking lot attendant?"

Before the rider could reply, the girl said, "Thanks for trying, Gary. I'm fine now. See you later, okay?"

"Sure . . . Sure. Maybe I'll see *you* later too." He tapped at Backer's chest. "If I find out what garage you hang out in."

"You can find him in class tomorrow at 9," ter Horst informed him, "if you manage to attend."

"This . . . old guy is a student?"

"If I can wedge my walker through the door, Young Blood." Backer's eyes were still on the girl in her VW.

Swearing, the boy moved off.

"Late again!" Ter Horst heaved to starboard.

"Aren't you always?" asked the girl.

"It's generally the productive who become preoccupied." He stumped away through the parking lot. "The idle have little to impede their punctuality—or their presumption."

They watched him go, an aging and slightly disrep-

utable lion. "You're one of his special ones, aren't you?"
she asked.

"He's . . . been very special to me."

"And you're a Christian too, aren't you?"

His reddish eyes stared into green ones. "Yes."

"It shows around the eyes somehow."

"You too."

"Not acting much like one these days." She sighed.
"Sometimes I wonder what's the use of me at all. After
twenty-two years—"

"And you're a biology major."

She was startled. "Have we met?"

"One time we had . . . a debate on the meaning of
life. A kind of . . . deep debate."

Abruptly she squealed, "Look at the *time*! Prof's not
the only white rabbit. If I miss my doctor's appointment
again, he'll— Maybe I'll see you again."

"Maybe," Backer said to the girl he had not seen
since that morning in the gulch as her little green bug put-
tered up the hill. "You never know who you'll see again.
You just never, ever know."

———

The Alexander home was a three-storied modified
colonial, past Colorado Boulevard in Denver.

Shown into the study by an elderly housekeeper,
Backer found Anna Alexander at her desk, hunched over
some lithographs. The Tiffany lamp above cast harsh shadows on her angular face. Behind her was a huge ebony cre-
denza topped by a Remington bronze.

She was the image of young Darcey, plus thirty years. Long horsey face, haunted blue eyes, ash-blonde hair, streaked with gray where it was swept back from the high temples.

"Please be seated, Mr. Backer." She went back to the study of her lithograph.

"Nice place, Mrs. Alexander." Backer shrugged his jacket off, pulled up a red velvet chair, and leaned back, cocking an eyebrow. "Dandy cowboy collection."

Her head jerked up.

"Those are Russells and Remingtons, primarily. Since you probably will not have a frequent opportunity to view them here, I'll have my secretary send you a schedule of their display dates at the Denver Art Museum."

Backer rocked the chair back, balancing on his toes. "Actually, I don't much like Old West American representational. All that grim macho stuff. For an expression of nineteenth century human beings trying to get the connection between our spiritual force and the elemental power of nature, I think guys like Turner and Constable finish in the money. They're just as high-handed, I guess, but a lot less uptight about what a friend of mine calls 'their mythopoeic pantheism.'"

There was a brass-studded footstool nearby, and Backer hooked it and dragged it under his boots. "Don't you think?"

Hard blue eyes blinked at him.

"Care for some cognac, Mister Backer? Or perhaps you'd prefer a Coors."

"Just black coffee would be peachy." Backer tipped back in his chair. "About a trough full. It was a long drive—in answer to your . . . summons."

"Mister Backer . . ." The tall woman pushed back

from her desk. "Though I regard your attempt to compare Russell with Turner as the most egregious fancy, it does suggest to me one or two things . . ."

There was a silence as the drinks were brought.

All this was only a variation, Backer realized as they sipped, of the predator-dance he had performed countless times on other turf. Different lyrics, same tune.

Anna Beaucage Alexander's steel-blue eyes contemplated Backer over the edge of her glass.

"Either," she mused, "you have gone to some trouble to disguise your sensibilities beneath those layers of muscle and leather, or you've done some homework. You have, I surmise, recently visited an art museum . . . or perhaps a library?"

Chuckling, Backer rested his head against the back of the velvet chair. "Dawn . . . she's a . . . a friend. She often talks to me about art."

Another sharp look. "You throw away your only advantage—mystery—quickly, though I still admire the tenacity you employed in preparing yourself. Was this your idea or ter Horst's? And did you understand anything you've said?"

"I learn from everybody, Mrs. Alexander. I'm learning from you. But my ideas are my own, and matter of fact my opinions are mine too. We've been to your museum here—I think it's great. But I don't like Russell or Remington, and I do like Turner and Constable."

Backer settled deep into his chair, putting down the cup. "And the guys like David and Ingre, the Neo-Classicists who came before 'em . . . They admired honor, discipline. Can't argue with that. Pity they had to be at war with the later guys just 'cause . . . well, 'cause they were later guys."

He smiled, the scar tissue knotting, exaggerating his grin. "My friend and I really do talk, you see."

Alexander was up, staring out the full-length window that led to her garden. "So the point of your little monologue is that the old and outdated must give way to the . . . current fashion, whatever it is."

"No," Backer answered, not rising. "My point was, maybe there is *more* . . . out there, in everything."

He looked up. "You think there's *more*, Mrs. Alexander?"

With a speed he would not have anticipated, the woman moved to stand in front of him. Lamplight made hollows below her cheekbones.

"I think there's more impudence in your hirsute Age of Aquarius. What are we calling ourselves this year? Jesus People, is it? Or Jesus Freaks? Or do you use a trendier, more mystical name?"

He twisted up out of his seat. "I use the name Clint Backer," he said extending his hand, "and I've met Someone using the name Christ. He is the force of the very real, the very personal God. I am His to use as He chooses."

The eyes of the two locked in the Tiffany glow. "But I'm still just . . . me," Backer added. "I don't handle snakes, I don't swing from chandeliers, and I roll down aisles only when I get *very* excited. All I do is read the Book, ask the Man, and follow Him. I think Darcey wants to try that road, if you'll let him."

Now there was a hand on his arm with strength in it.

"Why do you want my boy? Didn't I give enough when they used up my older son in Viet Nam? Why is Darcey changed? What are you after?"

Gently he lifted her fingers. "I'm after peace, Mrs.

Alexander. And maybe that god you call on so easily isn't the real one. But the real One wants Darcey. I don't—even though I have come to . . . yeah, to love him as a brother."

She whirled away. He followed, turned her.

They faced each other. "You're sharp," he said. "Try and get it. Darcey and me . . . we're part of a circle now. No better than we were before, but *He's* inside us."

He walked to the hall. "I'll see myself out, thank you so much."

She pursued him to the door. *"What are you going to do to my son?"*

"I'm going to be his friend, Mrs. Alexander. We might work on some cars together, and next Saturday we're kicking off a campus Bible study. We'll pray, and we'll sing some, them that can, and we'll ask God—the real One—to teach us. No—" He put forth a hand to forestall her interjection. "—we don't think we know everything . . . Or much. But we're going to learn. Since my only area of experience to date concerns people's amazing capacity to screw up, I suspect we'll probably do some of that too. And that covers it. Except for one thing—"

Grudgingly she watched him swing open the oak-paneled front door and swing aboard his bike.

"We expect Him to teach us about it all," he called, "the laws, the facts, the stuff you gotta know to survive in this place. You know—" He revved up the engine. "—the stuff a parent wants a child to know."

Expressionlessly, she watched from the hall as Backer coasted down the circular drive and out into the street.

"You're a skeptical woman," Backer called. "Why don't you come up and see for yourself?" His voice was diminishing with the distance. "Or have you lost your

instinct for knowing when the other side's bluffing and
when they've got the right cards?"

The oak door slammed shut, but the house had high
windows, and Backer felt eyes follow him all the way
down the street and around the corner.

———

Not long after, Darcey moved in with Clint and the
two found a small garage-apartment in Boulder. The stall
beneath quickly filled with vehicles in need of repair as
Darcey proved to have inherited the Beaucage-Alexander
business acumen. The pair quickly found themselves self-
supporting.

Both also carried maximum class loads. Backer was
unpolished, but his mind was awake and hungry, devour-
ing everything—theological and secular.

It did not come easily: he was older; he was a biker;
he was a Christian. But by summer's end he had carved out
his own niche.

The Bible studies were held on the quad in the warm-
ing summer evenings. They began as a devotional group,
but evolved into a society.

Lynne, the auburn-banged girl from Backer's past,
led many of the sessions. But she never connected him
with the drunken werewolf in the ditch, and he never
reminded her.

When Lynne began to have withdrawn spells, ter
Horst seemed to understand, but would not explain. With
the FishHouse still closed, the members began attending
the campus meetings. Niklhas led some, and so did Kobol.

Ter Horst would hold forth too. But by summer's end, to his own surprise, Backer emerged as leader.

Then Darcey's mother came. She sat quietly behind the group and spoke to no one but ter Horst.

Then she came again.

After the third visit, Darcey was absent from class for three days, staying in Denver with his mother. "Anna Beaucage Alexander," ter Horst pronounced, "is rapidly metamorphosing into a human being."

The last week of the summer semester, sitting cross-legged on the lawn, Backer's heavy brow was bent over First Thessalonians and a Greek lexicon. There were low murmurs about him as the company began to collect. A guitar twanged.

At the corner of his puckered left eye Backer saw a flash of yellow twirl toward him. Well-honed reflexes pulled his neck back, and a Frisbee swished by, missing him by millimeters. He heard the snap as someone behind him snatched it.

"Excuse," said the catcher.

"Okay."

The disc swished overhead again, brushing Clint's hair.

His arm darted up, snagging the thing out of the sky. "Hey!"

He flipped the Frisbee to the other man. "Mind taking it down the road a piece? We're expecting company."

"You having a convention?"

"Chill it, man," his friend called. It was Gary, Lynne's letter-jacket, non-mechanical friend.

"That's old Father Backer. A whole flock of woolly baa-baa's must be right behind. Let's oblige the man and move down."

Father Backer. Clint sighed.

"Do Christians get the blues?" he asked himself, knowing the answer.

But that day turned into a surprisingly good session. Towards the close, Lynne, who had been silent throughout, asked, "Anybody thinking about the big concert this fall?" She pointed at a poster pinned to a tree.

Celebrate Halloween Early with the Greatest Rock and Roll Band Alive, it demanded. Beneath the legend was a photo of a lean, prancing man frozen in mid-scream.

"At Red Rocks Amphitheater," Lynne went on.

Chavez sauntered up to the poster. "Heavy sounds, heavy stoners." He glanced at Lynne. "You really think we should infiltrate this gig?"

"What does anybody think?" Backer asked.

"*I* think they *are* the best band alive," interjected Darcey.

"Except for the drummer, who O.D.'d last year," said Niklhas.

Kobol sprawled on the grass. "Without the Main Man, we're all as dead as their last drummer."

"I met a man at a concert once," Backer said quietly. "What he said about the Man didn't take right away, but later—"

"We should go," Lynne repeated, her face strangely pale beneath the unusually scraggly bangs.

Backer noticed the thinning hair and the bright spots on the girl's cheeks. He put it down to a summer cold.

"So what do we do?" asked Dawn.

"It's not what we do, it's what we are," Backer answered. "Go without judgment, but with love. Be ready to talk if a door opens. That's it, chillen. That's the whole of it."

———

The subject of the concert seldom came up again, as Lynne appeared less and less frequently in their group. It was understood that she was struggling to achieve her diploma by the end of Summer Session, and her absence was laid to that.

When the fellowship held an early-September party in her honor, she was distracted and indistinct about her future plans.

Busy with his own preparation for the autumn semester, Backer gave her reticence little thought. But while he was flipping through the C.U. fall catalogue one evening, trying without success to locate any listing for a class led by ter Horst, the phone rang.

Darcey held the receiver. "It's ter Horst," he said, and something in his voice made Backer's head snap up.

"He wants you at the campus hospital. Lynne's dying."

———

Ter Horst stood outside the door of Room 321.

"Breast cancer. Chemotherapy failed. Mastectomy last year only slowed it. They don't think she'll last the night."

"You never told us."

"It was her life, and she lived it her way. She wanted to be treated like everybody else . . . to the last. She went from clinic to school to dorm and back."

The room smelled of old flowers and death.

"Clint?"

He took her small white hand. "We could pray. We could ask—"

"I've already asked. He's calling me Home." She smiled, eyelids closed. "I want to go."

"Not very considerate of the rest of us. We'll complain to the management."

A whisper of a laugh. "Like *you've* got a complaint . . . Only twenty-three years, and when I go, it'll be like pulling a finger out of the sea . . . A ripple, and *poof* . . . now you see her, now you don't."

"Lynne, you've meant so much to so many—"

Her hand fluttered up, fingers to his lips. "Big tough Clint . . . Always up front . . . out there . . . on the streets . . . in the classes. How many have been fished out of the darkness because of you? Darcey, Nora, Kelley, maybe Anna—who knows? How many more after that before—" Her voice died.

Suddenly Backer was aware of the electronic beep of the bedside machine as the white dot on its screen went up and down, tracing her final moments.

Brisk footsteps in the hall. Urgently Backer spoke her name. Her eyes flickered open.

A nurse's voice. "Sir, you'll have to—"

"Lynne, listen—" He was willing the words into her consciousness. "I—"

Another nurse was in the room, and they were pushing past him. "Mister, you've got to—"

"Look at me! *I was the man in the gulch that night.*"

For a moment her eyes fastened on his. "Then . . . there *was* a reason."

Hands were shoving him away. Shouted orders mingled with the sudden shriek of the machine as the white dot ceased its tracing of peaks and valleys and slid into a smooth white line, smooth as Lynne's face as her eyes closed and her smile faded.

Backer was pushed out the door just before it slammed. Putting his hand to its laminated surface he said, "Lynne, thank you."

Then he said good-bye.

THE HOUSE

On a dull rainy afternoon a week after Lynne's funeral, the thunder over Backer's Boulder apartment was pierced by a call from Mrs. Alexander.

"Come see me at my newspaper office . . . Fifteenth Street."

"There's a cloudburst over Boulder."

"It's raining in Denver too. You should expect to get wet if you ride a Marley."

"Harley."

"Yes. Wear that brigand's jacket . . . I assume it's water-repellent."

"Mmmm—"

"It's certainly repellent in all other respects. And bring my son."

"Why can't it wait?"

"How many things can, actually?"

Backer hung up the phone.

"Why does Mom want to talk to you and not me? And what's she want?"

"Her own way." Backer sighed. "A summons from the Queen of Diamonds."

Flipping up their collars, Backer and Darcey rode the Harley through the sheets of rain to Denver.

In her top-floor office Mrs. Alexander rose to greet them.

Darcey peered over her shoulder, out the droplet-tracked window. The big tires of a cream-color Caddy splashed into gutter water at curbside several stories below.

"Uh-huh . . . Your chariot awaits. What's the plan, Mommy Machiavelli, ma'am?"

"Darcey, don't be impertinent," she snapped. "If you've inherited any sense at all from the Beaucage side of the family, you'll ride with me. You look like a lonesome guppy."

"Where do you plan on taking this gruesome puppy?" asked Backer as she swept past him to the door.

"Guppy. And please, Clint, spare us that dreadful sound you believe is a chuckle. Considering your current resemblance to a drowned alley cat, I suggest you join us."

There was plenty of room in the rear of the well-insulated limo. Liquid machine-gun fire rattled over its roof.

"The Eagleton place please, Danny."

Nodding, the chauffeur wheeled out into the scattered traffic, slid right on Broadway, left on 11th, and right again on Logan. They swung in beside a granite edifice brooding over the corner of the hill that swelled up Logan.

As Backer climbed out the door, he looked past dripping elms sprouting out from the curbside strip of grass, shadowing the old wide, cracked sidewalk.

Beyond the walk was a yard-high stone retaining wall topped by a fence of black iron spears. There was an inset six-foot gate five steps up.

"Are the Munsters expecting callers?" Backer followed the others through the squealing gate.

Mrs. Alexander did not deign to reply, but walked briskly toward the old place. The rain persuaded Darcey to follow.

Using a hand to shield his face from the driving rain, Clint surveyed the grounds. The main building, he saw, was an ancient stone rectangle, three stories in some places, four in others, two at the ends. The lawn was wide and green, and he could just make out blurred edges of outbuildings where the ground in back began its upward slope.

Mrs. Alexander hurried onto the veranda between two of the six columns that supported the roof into which an eagle with a nine-foot wingspread had been chiseled.

"This," she said to Darcey and Backer as they scrambled to join her in the shelter beneath the eagle's talons, "does not fall into the category of choice real estate, despite its central location."

She nodded to where the capitol dome was visible, its golden surface glistening in the rain. "Only a few blocks from downtown, this area is full of massive old houses, mostly fallen into neglect."

Backer suddenly realized that they were within walking distance of the burned-out remains of the FishHouse.

Chattering like a sales agent, Mrs. Alexander put a long hand on an ornate knob below a tremendous oval of stained glass.

"Zoned both residential and commercial, it retains much of the original furnishings. It was leased to a fraternity—as you'll see by the atrocious murals."

"Mom, could you 'cut to the chase'?" Darcey shook the water from his yellow hair.

"Once this was the home of Charlotte Eagleton."

Darcey snapped his fingers. "Haunted Hill! No wonder it's vacant . . . Is it one of yours?"

Mrs. Alexander twisted the brass knob. "It was picked up by some fool in my investment company . . . and it hasn't found a buyer. But it's no longer vacant, and it's no longer mine."

The wind was whipping up. "Then who—" Darcey shuddered as the rain pelted him again.

"It's ours." Niklhas, framed in soft light from the hall, swung wide the glass-paneled door. "Welcome home, folks."

———

Sliding down the dark winding banister, past the portraits and the mounted birds, Darcey shouted, "Hitchcock should see this. Alfie would be very much at home."

"Somebody should," Backer muttered into his coffee cup as he sat on the old wingback sofa with Darcey's mother and Dawn. Niklhas faced them from the depths of a red leather armchair. A small fire crackled below the carved hearth, outlining his perfect profile.

". . . a foundation," he was saying. "Mrs. Alexander's attorney is pushing through the paperwork. We'll be a non-profit corporation. This place has rooms for the homeless, storage for food, clothing, a place for workshops—anything."

"And a board of Denver's sharpest business people to watchdog the integrity of the operation," Dawn added. "They're instructing me in what they call 'resource development'—raising money, to you plebes."

Mrs. Alexander nodded. "It's a tax write-off for me, and you'll be eligible for government grants with your house in order."

"And you run the house?" Backer asked.

"No." Niklhas shook his head. "I do. Mrs. Alexander chairs the board, but the president will ramrod the operation."

"Good luck." Backer was staring at the cartoonish wall murals—imitation Greek frescoes, mementos of the house's time as a fraternity, as were the red English pay-telephone booths scattered throughout the building.

"And I'm secretary-treasurer." Dawn smiled. "All we need is a vice president and we're in business."

The flames popped. Everyone waited for Backer to speak.

After a pause Mrs. Alexander said, "My newspapers will cover your progress. I had your work investigated very thoroughly—including statistics on the rehabilitation of those you've 'converted.'" She glanced at Darcey as he sauntered into the room. "I must say, I'm convinced. You've—you've made a believer of me again."

"It's not us you should believe in," Backer said quietly.

"Of course not. Don't presume to lecture me, Clint Backer. It's the One behind you in whom I've come to trust."

"What room did Ambrose Eagleton hang himself in?" Darcey asked.

His mother frowned, then spoke over the ensuing hubbub. "Charlotte Eagleton was a strongly . . . religious woman." She sighed. "In the sense I used to be, I suppose . . . wrapping the gospel around her own strong will, to enforce her opinions. Naturally—" She glanced at Darcey.

"—her son rebelled. Ambrose Eagleton became notorious as the leader of a cult involved in all sorts of bizarre practices. He succumbed to depression. One night a maid discovered him in his room, hanging from a rafter. Don't ask . . . I've no intention of identifying that room for you."

"It does seem . . . heavy in here." Dawn shivered. "I thought it was just the age of the house."

"Oppression," Niklhas agreed. "But it doesn't matter how dark it's gotten here . . . We're bringing the Light."

"A Communion service," said Backer.

They turned to him.

"What?"

Backer stood, looking down into the fire. "This weekend . . . everybody . . . the whole FishHouse circle." He squinted into the flames. "We're not gonna leave the darkness a clawhold."

Dawn hit the arm of the couch, raising dust. "Out of the dust God makes the best.'"

"The FishHouse . . . from the ashes, like a phoenix," laughed Darcey.

"Not a phoenix." Backer looked away from the hearth. "An eagle." Softly he quoted, "'I will rise up . . . on eagle's wings.'"

Niklhas uncoiled, stretched his huge frame. "Weekend will come soon," he said. "Let's get Eagle's Wing ready."

———

A week of scrubbing, waxing, painting, cleaning. Darcey, Niklhas, and Backer stayed at the place;

Dawn lived with Mrs. Alexander. The girl had begun to function as the heiress' assistant, and it appeared to Backer that the two were drawing close. Both women joined other fellowship members in working on the old place in the evenings.

The night before the gathering, Backer clung to a stepladder, repairing shelves in the second-floor library.

He liked the room. Its shelves had been stocked with contributions from everyone in the fellowship, including ter Horst. When combined with volumes left by the Eagletons and the fraternity, its catalogue ranged from Socrates to Spinoza to Spiderman.

A different kind of collection had been gathered by Darcey. In the musty basement he discovered a 1955 Rockola jukebox, another legacy from the departed fraternity. In ecstasy he cajoled Nik, Backer, Chavez, and Kobol into helping him heave it up into the wide drawing room, where his busy fingers quickly brought it to neon-flickering operational life.

He stocked it with the folk-rock of the late sixties, though Dawn had insisted on adding what classical pieces she could find on 45 rpm.

Now the gentle harmonies of Peter, Paul, and Mary floated into the library.

Below the ladder, Dawn rubbed vigorously at the patina on an antique globe, working by touch and instinct. Backer could smell the strawberry-like aroma of her copper hair.

"How do you know what to do?" he asked as he fit a teak shelf into place.

"Common sense, acquired knowledge, and a kind of inner knowing . . . like Christianity." She put down the Pledge and gave the globe a spin.

"I wish . . . *I* knew what to say . . . right now."

"You?" She laughed. "You always seem to know what to say and do, Clint. I think you're a natural."

"I think you're beautiful."

"Thank you." Her hands stopped the globe's spin.

"I love you, Dawn."

"I love you too, Clint. And I know you're beautiful."

"No . . . But . . . you really do love—"

"That's why I want to tell you first. We're going to announce it to everybody tomorrow . . . Nik and I are engaged."

Backer worked on the shelf. "Of course," he said, "of course you are."

———

That night, in the small bedroom he had chosen under the eaves, Clint stayed awake a long time.

Afterwards he was never sure what disturbed the sleep into which he finally drifted. But suddenly he seemed to be sitting up, shivering. Outside, charcoal-smoke clouds curled past the moon. Bedroom shadows shifted.

Something moved in the corner. For a moment it had looked like a face—swollen with self-pity, dead, twisting, suspended by a cord from the rafters in the corner of the room.

By reflex, even before he was awake enough to hit the light switch, he had begun to gently pray.

There was, of course, nothing there. But he knew he had chosen the small bedroom where Ambrose Eagleton had decided to end his life in sorrow and denial. He knew too the supreme power and presence of his Lord, Jesus Christ.

———

They were all there for the first gathering that chilly late-September evening: Chavez, Kobol, Nora, ter Horst, Darcey and his mother, and thirty others. They sat in heavy old chairs, scattered over the Persian carpet, crowding the wingback sofa, all across the high-ceilinged drawing room.

Members of the newly-christened Eagle's Wing passed the loaf of fresh-baked French bread, twisted loose a chunk, handed it on.

"'This is My body. Take, eat—'" Niklhas spoke the words as the first strains of a Bach harpsichord piece jangled from the flashing jukebox by the door. He took a bottle from the mantel, and while firelight glinted off its faceted surface, he poured purple liquid into lead crystal goblets that had been withdrawn from a cupboard and scoured spotless.

"'For this is my blood, shed for you. Do this, in remembrance of Me.'"

As Backer raised the glass to his lips he thought he saw an odd shadow waver in the silver surface of the mirror above the mantel. For a moment it was if he saw again the face from his dream: Ambrose Eagleton, bloated with despair. Then it trembled and became the face of Colt, eyes filled with anguish.

Backer drank, and as soft prayer and music rose about him, the image changed. He saw—or remembered—Lynne—pale, sinking, yet somehow vital, even as her face smoothed in death.

Lastly he thought he saw another face: bearded, dark, glowing with compassion. There was the reflection of a hand reaching out, a wound in its center.

It was his own hand as he raised a Bible and read, "'And the Light came into the darkness, and the darkness could not overcome it.'"

Backer knew he would be having no more dreams of Ambrose Eagleton, or of Colt. Nor would there be any more darkness in this house.

———

Before they broke up that night, Backer unrolled the poster announcing the coming concert at Red Rocks.

"Lynne's idea," Darcey said.

"And we're still going . . . For Lynne." Backer rolled up the poster.

Everyone agreed but ter Horst.

"Not your bag, huh, Dutch?" Chavez asked.

"Bags are what I carry home from Safeway. But in answer to your ill-phrased query, *Señor* Chavez, I'm not offering to spearhead your assault because I will not be here."

"No classes . . . It's a weekend," Darcey said.

"I shall not be in the country. I postponed my sabbatical until after Lynne's demise. I wanted to see—" He stopped. "Well, while you are mingling among the hard-rock heathen I will be scrambling between rocks and hard places in the city of Petra."

"You really leaving?" Niklhas asked.

"For a year . . . A tour of the Mediterranean and the Near East."

"But you've always been here," complained Kobol.

"Nothing here is forever," ter Horst sighed. "Didn't you learn *anything* in my classes?"

"Then we're—" Darcey began.

"We is on our own," Kobol interjected. "Merlin done split from Camelot."

"I like the allusion," chuckled ter Horst. "Yes, Logres will have to struggle on without the counsel contained within this hoary head. But to continue your metaphor, you've still got Arthur and Guinevere—" He inclined his bushy head at Niklhas and Dawn, who sat holding hands before the fire. "And Lancelot—"

Backer leaned against the flashing jukebox.

Ter Horst was silent a moment. "The story will turn out better this time, with God's grace."

While the others discussed the concert, Niklhas gestured to Backer. They spoke in the silence of the library.

"You sure you want to do this?" He unrolled the concert poster. The singer was still frozen in mid-scream.

Backer nodded.

"Clint, did you read it all?"

Backer took the edge of the poster in his fingers. At the bottom, in small letters, was the legend, *A FaveRock Production.*

The festival in Texas. The setup. The raid. Favereu, Blackburn, and Aikens in their underwear, tied to chairs, screaming while the Wolves roared into the night loaded with drugs and cash.

"Things do get curioser and curioser." Backer stared at the poster.

"You still going?"

In answer Backer slapped the globe as he passed it, sending it spinning. He went back to the drawing room, where plans were being laid for the concert.

13

THE CONCERT

The day of the concert was unseasonably warm. In the hours before the journey, Backer knelt over the pool behind the Logan Street house, pouring chlorine into the rippling waters.

"A baptismal service on Halloween." Niklhas shook his head. "We are in danger of unorthodoxy, if not outright hedonism."

"Can't think of a better way to spend tomorrow night." Backer stood up. "It'd be something to see . . . Somehow I don't think I'm gonna see it."

Niklhas squinted his cop's eyes at Backer. "If not tomorrow, you'll see it some other time. You'll be back here with us."

Backer plunked the chlorine jar on a shelf. "Sure I will."

Niklhas's hand rested on Backer's bare shoulder. "Ride easy, Ace. Remember, the D.A.'s office knows what you did at Favereu's Galveston festival. But Favereu isn't going to admit it, and neither would the Wolves. Anyway, word is, Aubrey's in deep with the mob. Cops are almost ready to nail him. Nobody's interested in you. You're history."

"Never could get through history." Backer started for the house to shower.

That bright afternoon Backer mounted his Harley as soon as Kobol's Winnebago lumbered into view. He waved his arm and shouted like Ward Bond on "Wagon Train": "Waa-gons . . . roll!"

The caravan snaked over the hills, Backer in the lead, Kobol at the rear. In between was the new bus—on lease from the Alexander organization, assorted vans and station wagons, Chavez mounted on a shiny black Honda C B 750, and Darcey traveling alongside on a golden Triumph 650, altogether too much like the machine Colt had ridden.

The Red Rocks outdoor amphitheater, carved out of hillside stone, host to everything from rock concerts to Easter services, was packed when they reached it that October afternoon.

The music beat down on them as they split up, then moved through the dancing, cheering crowd. Backer watched money and dope—acid was the drug of choice just then, though the market in mescaline and amphetamines was almost equally brisk—pass from hand to hand. He wondered if Favereu was involved in that end of the day's proceedings. Shielding his eyes against the lights, he could see the lot where the trailer with the *FaveRock Enterprises* banner was parked.

Should he move that way? That would be asking for trouble. Besides, it was late, and the day's celebration was drawing to a close.

"Can I give you this?" Somebody up ahead was handing out one of the pamphlets the group had ordered.

Backer and Dawn had picked them out—she listening for a polished turn of phrase, he for a realistic awareness of the people it would reach.

The lights were in his eyes, and he couldn't tell which of his people it was. It might have been Chavez, for the man was dark, but larger . . . And the voice—

An odd tingle went down Backer's spine. He moved through the crowd, blinking against the sun.

"I think I know you, but—"

"We're brothers at any rate." The man pointed to the small gold cross Backer wore around his neck.

"I guess a lot of us here are. My name's Backer "

"Yes. A very large man was needing you, over there." A hand pointed toward the FaveRock headquarters.

Niklhas. "He say why?"

". . . important."

Clint heard the last word. He looked back from the trailer, but the man was gone, the crowd closing in thickly over the route he must have taken.

With a shrug Backer made his way to the trailer, throwing on the leather jacket against the cool of the evening. Where a wolf's-head had once snarled across its back, the emblem of a fist was now sewn, with the index finger jutting skyward. Beneath it was the motto, *One Way*.

Outside the trailer he froze, recognizing the string-thin shape of Harry Blackburn, Favereu's lieutenant, whom Backer had left tied to a chair, screaming for revenge, the night of the Galveston festival.

Instinctively the rider turned away.

Blackburn paused with his hand on the trailer door. His dark glasses leveled at the *One Way* emblem. "More of you guys. Why doncha leave us alone? I hope you paid your way in at least."

Clint looked directly into Blackburn's lenses.

"G'wan," Blackburn said without a hint of recognition, "I got bidness."

The trailer door slammed.

Backer stood, rubbing his beard.

Nowhere could he make out Niklhas's big frame.

Then, from inside the trailer, he heard a familiar voice.

"You stupids . . . We just come for the fun today, thassall. Didn't even know you was here." There was a grunt of pain.

There was a glint of light between the curtain and trailer window. Backer pressed his face to it. Godzilla, the three-hundred-pound biker, was strapped to a chair, cords cutting into the thick flesh of his upper arms.

Blackburn brought the short barrel of his 9 mm. Baretta down across Godzilla's grizzled cheek.

"Don't give us that. In Galveston you ripped off our stash, our cash, and that cassette Rex was dumb enough to leave in the office machine. The Feds already got Rex in the stone hotel, and we don't plan to visit. Where's the tape?"

"Whatta you guys care?" Godzilla spat blood. "We don't want cops anymore 'n you."

Favereu grabbed the bigger man by the beard. "Because some of our people were *very* angry. You must be back for some reason. If that tape's still around—"

"Us Wolves gots better things to do than keep track of some bunch of tape."

Favereu slapped him. "Get the Pentathol."

Blackburn yanked open a panel in the trailer's side and withdrew a syringe and a bottle.

Favereu began filling the hypo. "With this we can be

pretty sure of the truth. But don't be wiggly or I'll get nervous and they'll find you with your brain fried."

He grabbed Godzilla's arm and thrust in the needle. "Maybe they will anyway." His thumb started to push the plunger.

With an explosion of glass, Backer's boot shattered the window. He somersaulted in, knocking the syringe from Favereu's fingers. Another twist and he was reaching for Blackburn's gun.

But the little barrel was pointing at his face. Backer froze.

"I know you," Harry ejaculated. "It was you who—"

And then he squeaked as the tip of a blade pressed against his throat.

"Let's drop our nasty toy." Roper's smoky voice coiled through the room as he dug the knife into Blackburn's neck.

Harry dropped the weapon. Backer picked it up, snapped out the clip, and pocketed it. "That's one I owe you, Rope."

"Just makes us even, Clint. Remember Galveston?"

"Backer!" Godzilla shouted from his chair. "Whoo-eeee! I thought you was bad-lookin' before, but you gone and dipped your head in some ugly."

"Love you too, Godz."

The three-hundred-pounder lumbered to his feet as Roper slit his bonds.

"Not again," whimpered Favereu. "Please . . . the insurance didn't cover the last trailer you busted up. I was in the hospital for weeks with bleeding ulcers."

The two bikers led Aubrey and Harry gently to the sofa and pushed them down.

"Now follow me on this," Roper began patiently,

leaning on his thighs, "we ain't got no tape no more. It's prob'ly lyin' in the desert somewhere twixt here and Oakland. We don't want cops, we don't want big trouble." He took Harry's face in his hands. "Now we got places to go. But if you ever *ever* hassle us again—well—" Leaning over, he placed a wet, Bugs Bunny, smacking kiss on Harry's forehead above his dark glasses. "You'll go the way I hear poor Rex went last year. You play in the fast lane, you gotta watch out for faster rigs."

"Aubrey," Backer asked, "do you know the story of Odysseus and Polyphemus?"

"I haven't got time or energy for Polly Parrot stories," Aubrey moaned.

"No, I found this out in class." Backer leaned down over the promoter and ruffled his hair.

"See, Polyphemus was this Cyclops dude . . . one-eyed."

"You want me to hire the handicapped?"

"It couldn't hurt. But the point being, this Cyclops, he could only see things one way . . . his way."

"I'm not going to like this."

"A true word from a false man. Anyhow, our hero Odysseus poked Poly's eye out and got his whole crew away."

"Charming."

"I'm sure his people appreciated it. But then, you know what—while they were splitting, Odysseus had the impudence—*hubris* the Greeks called it—pride against the gods—to swagger, boast, and generally ignore reality."

"Are you talking me to death?"

"Almost done . . . And you been walking dead a long spell, so hush yourself up. So Odysseus was cursed by the high muckamucks to wander the earth before he found home and hearth."

Aubrey's head hung over his chest, and a vein in his temple throbbed. "The moral being?"

"Being that it's good to know when to shut up, take the money, and run."

Bending down, he patted Favereu's shoulder. "Run, ol' boy. Run while you can. Or else stand quiet and face the truth."

"I don't want truth. I don't want you . . . ever again. Let me run my sets . . . do my deals. That's all, please."

"I'll let you, but you'll run your back against the wall, Aubrey ol' boy. Trust me on this one. You'll want help."

"My attorney in Beverly Hills is the best."

For a moment Backer thought of the police and remembered Niklhas's words. He left the trailer with the certainty he would not be seeing anyone from FaveRock Enterprises ever again.

As the riders left the trailer, Backer looked around at the still-sitting promoters. "Incidentally," he said, "about last year . . . I'm sorry."

They stared. Godzilla laughed as he hopped down the steps. Roper looked at Backer as if seeing him for the first time.

"You *have* changed." They climbed the steps toward the main parking lot. "Let's go see if Wulff recognizes you."

There was a coldness in Backer's stomach as he followed his friends.

Most of the gang had already gone, but a half-dozen Wolves still straddled their machines in the milling crowds of the parking lot.

Wulff stared into Backer's eyes for a moment, then gave his long, slow, distinctive smile, showing his canines.

"Deacon said he saw you in Denver with a crowd a'

prime hookers hangin' on you like hounds on a steak bone. I knew that was my ol' Scout."

"S' not like you think, Wulff—Good to see you—Those girls were listening to me. I told 'em that—"

For the first time Godzilla saw the back of Clint's jacket.

"Wunn way," Godzilla read "Whassat mean, Backer? Where's yer wulf's-head?"

"That means I found the answer, Godz. I really did."

"What . . . um . . . what was the question?"

"Question is," Wulff said very quietly, "where's your wolf?"

"What did you find, Backer?" Roper asked.

"Christ . . . Jesus."

Silence.

"Sure . . . Jesus Gonzales." Porky laughed. "Remember? Runs a taco stand outsida Taos."

"I found God. Turns out He's alive and—this'll blow you away, Rope—He loves you . . . Just like you are."

Godzilla's mouth hung open. "He loves *Roper*?"

Wulff cut off Roper's objection. "So you got no more use for your old friends?"

"You're my oldest friend, Wulff. But I got Somebody I want you to meet. He sticks even closer than a brother."

"You were runnin' a little shy of brothers last time around." Backer's color deepened, and Wulff moved in a step. "But old friends are the best, and you took an oath, old friend."

"And you broke it," Deacon said, moving up with Porky and several others to surround Backer.

"So I took an oath to the Devil to stay in Hell." Slowly he looked around the closing circle. "I'm just not crazy anymore, guys."

"So now I'm Satan, am I?" Wulff hissed.

Backer staggered, bumped from behind. He swiveled and was bumped again.

"Please . . ." He caught his balance. "Just give me one chance to tell you."

He was bumped a third time, pitching forward into Spyder.

"We'd love to hear ya." Spyder dug his hook into the leather of Backer's jacket, lifting him up. "But there's just so many of us and so one of you that we're just not gonna hear you."

"What with the screams and all." Porky spun him around.

"Then we'll pass it on until everybody hears." A deep voice brought their heads around. Kobol moved out from behind a pickup, black biceps glistening below his white T-shirt.

"Maybe we'll sing it in harmony, so you can really listen." Niklhas stepped around a Dodge station wagon and put a hand out to steady Backer.

Godzilla spat tobacco. "They grows 'em big up here, don't they?"

"You found yourself some funny playmates." Wulff looked from Kobol to Niklhas.

"I'm a six-pack of laughs all by myself, *vato*," Chavez rasped, suddenly crouched on the hood of a beige Duster.

"Reminds me of me when I was meaner," muttered Roper.

Abruptly Wulff turned on his heel and swung aboard his machine. "So maybe we don't talk just now. Tell you what—" The bike screamed into life, joined by the roar of the others. "You come pay us a call."

"For tricks and treats," Porky yelled.

"We got us a Halloween party comin' up tomorrow." Wulff revved up. "The band's staked in that old mining camp we went through last year—just above Central City."

"Plenty touristy chicks, comin' to see the bandits." Porky laughed.

Wulff rolled forward until his front tire was nudging Backer. "Follow the trail of booze and broads and busted-up stuff. When you get to the end of it, we'll be there. You come and tell us all about what you found. Just come alone."

His machine raised up in a grandstanding wheelie, and he screeched across the lot, followed by the riders, his last words hanging in the air.

"Alone . . . If you still got the blood in your veins for it."

"Yeah, Wulff." Backer watched them go. "I got the blood. But I'm not alone . . . Not anymore."

THE CAMP

Sunset, October 31, 1970. Still warm.

An argument burst out inside the Eagle's Wing library, where the fellowship was gathered around the long conference table.

"You're wrong!" Darcey shouted. "Going in there alone, it'll be lions versus Christians all over again!"

"Wolves, not lions," Backer replied from the opposite end of the table. "And they've got mighty empty bellies."

"It's you they'll ingest, old son," said Kobol.

Backer walked away from the table, looked out the window at the lengthening shadows, and leaned on the sill.

"They're hurting. Their souls are . . . like darkness and caves of ice." His reddish eyes found Niklhas. "You're the one who said we should bring 'em the Light."

"*I'm* the one saying you got a death wish!" Darcey blurted, stomping out of the room. The door slammed. A moment later the sound of the jukebox blared through the paneling.

"If you have to go, Clint, don't go alone." Dawn leaned forward, her elbows on the table.

"Who would I take?" Backer stepped forward again. "Nik? He's got the baptismal service tonight; he's gotta be there. Anna's papers have PR'd it. Eagle's Wing is on its way."

His glance covered the room. "Dawn?"

She lowered her sightless violet eyes. "I'd be no good there."

"Not one of the women," agreed Backer. "Not up there . . . not tonight."

"They ain't doin' nothin' I ain't done before, honey," Nora growled.

"Sorry, Big Blonde." Backer smiled. "Not this time."

"Maybe," Kobol mused, "I could get my sister-in-law to take the kids to that party—"

"They go with Dad." Backer walked to the door. "And Chavez is out running the shuttle bus, collecting the new ones for tonight. You guys got your work here."

He opened the door. "And out there is mine. I see that now."

"Clint!" snapped Niklhas. The rider turned, shutting the door against the Rockola's blare.

"We can be with you in prayer anyhow."

Niklhas at his right, Kobol at his left, the circle was made. Prayer, silent and spoken, rose softly, blotting out the old Rockola's buzz.

Next door, bathed in the old jukebox's garish neon glow, Darcey put head on arm on the machine and offered his private supplications.

"I'm going," Backer finally said, breaking the circle. "But I'm not really traveling alone." He went through the door. "We all know that."

The rest of the circle stayed in the room, in the lamp-light, listening to the buzz of Backer's Harley as he rolled down Logan and started the long trek to the old mining camp above Central City.

Already little trick-or-treaters were pattering up the street. As Backer turned onto 11th, he could still hear the music emanating from the Eagle's Wing, and he smiled when he placed the tune Darcey had punched out. It was "Monster Mash."

———

Nightfall settled into the hills before he reached Central City. He pulled over at The Glory Hole, a place that held good memories for him, and had a Coke.

"Know about any bikers camped around here?" he asked the old man who brought his drink.

"Yeah . . . They been in. Know better than to raise a ruckus 'round here. But they dropped word they got an all-night Halloween bash goin', an' a few tourist types even got costumes." He sniffed. "I locked my daughter up tonight."

Refreshing his memory with a set of directions to the cluster of tumbled-down shacks that surrounded the played-out silver mine, Backer climbed the hills through the thickening darkness.

At last, above him, at the crest of the trail, he recognized a tree: an old oak, blackened by lightning, little more than a nine-foot chunk of wood with two thick branches stretching crookedly out from either side, approximately parallel. It had been dead a long time. Legend called it The Lynching Tree, where miners' justice—and more than a few miners—had been executed.

As he rolled abreast, he noticed that boxes and barrels, evidently pilfered from the ghost town below, had been stacked higgledy-piggledy about the base of the tree, so that a life-size dummy could be suspended from one of the gnarled branches. Somebody's flannel shirt and jeans, stuffed with trash, swung in the breeze, while a gigantic pumpkin head, a thick piece of wood connecting it to the body, hung by its "neck."

Its face was cut into an anguished scream, and the burning candle within sent hellfire blazing from its eyes.

Backer pushed his Harley forward and glided down the slope into camp.

He rumbled by a cavern entrance, over the remains of ore-car track that protruded from the shaft. Ahead were a dozen dilapidated structures: stables, small houses, a general store, a saloon with one faded-green bat-wing door sagging by a single hinge.

Around the well, in the center of the street, dozens of bikes and black-and-silver vans were scattered.

At the far edge of town Backer spotted the scarlet bonfire that cut through the mountain blackness. He saw dancers' silhouettes, some obviously in outlandish costume.

He stopped the Harley, swung down the kickstand, and made his way to the fire and the noise.

A girl Backer did not know bumped against him, sloshing beer. He moved her gently aside.

Porky, in a Dracula cape and devil horns, waved to him from his seat by the fire. "Bless me, father, for I am stoned."

Shannon, Wulff's woman, came up to him. Her ironed-straight silver hair and gray eyes contrasted vividly with her black, low-cut vampire gown.

"Hello, Clint. You back with the pack?"

Smiling, he shook his head. "Found a new road. Gonna take my whole life to follow the trail."

"That's too long for anything." She put her hand against his chest.

"Not for this. I want to let the pack in on it."

"Why not let me in on it?" Then she took her hand away. "You look different. And it ain't just the beard or the burn. You've changed somehow."

Spyder, gaunt and drawn, stumbled into him. "Woo-hoo . . . Hally-looya. That old-time religion got our Scout."

"No, Spyder, Jesus Christ got me."

"Scout is back, and God's got him! Hey, you can reel 'im in with this. Recollect it?" His hook held a rusty chain. "I won it offa Deacon." The biker giggled. "From Colt's ol' Triumph, remember?" He swung it overhead. "Handy in a hassle."

"Wear it in good health, man." Backer moved on to confront Wulff, who sat on the far edge of the fire.

"'Lo, Preacher," Wulff said as Backer slid down the side of a ruined mine shack to squat beside him. "Colt snuffed, you split, the party ain't been the same."

"Things change, Wulff."

"Not here, they don't. Everything's just like it was five, six years ago. You recall that time we—"

"Look"—Backer nodded at Spyder, who stumbled about, almost falling in the fire—"see those lines in his face? And his size . . . Man, he used to weigh twenty, thirty pounds more."

Wulff shrugged. "It's the speed. Eats him up, but it gets him happy."

"He's not getting happy . . . He's getting old."

The bottle of Southern Comfort in Wulff's hand flew past Backer's face to smash within the circle of fire. Blue flames spit upward.

"Nobody's old. Old don't exist here."

Sliding a finger across Wulff's coarse black hair where it bunched out from beneath the red bandanna, Backer murmured, "You got some gray hair, man."

Wulff's hands dug into Backer's jacket, pulling him close. "And you could have a new face, old friend."

Backer easily removed the big fists from his leather. "I got a new face. Didn't you notice?"

Riders were drifting around now.

"Tell you what else I got . . . I got free."

Roper chewed the end of a stick, took it out to look at it with his sleepy eyes, then tossed it into the fire. "You come on real heavy with that Jesus jive."

"Just because He . . . uh, like . . ." Backer sighed. "He's strong inside me, real strong. But I don't want to come down heavy. Y' know, I'm still new at this. Don't want to give anybody a hard time."

Roper chuckled. "A Backer who doesn't wanna give anybody hard times. That's a miracle right there."

Wulff growled.

"Roper, why don't you look at me?" Backer put a hand on the lean rider's arm.

Sharply Roper looked up, then snapped, "Why do you keep pushing it?"

"For the first time that I can think . . ." Backer groped for words. ". . . I'm happy, man. That's all. I'm . . . just . . . happy."

For a long time they listened. First one, then two, then a heavy portion of the pack split away from the dance at the fire's edge and knelt or stood by Backer, though many ignored him or even shouted insults.

Finally the conversation was cut short by Wulff, who leaned forward and shoved Roper hard. He toppled backwards, close to the blaze.

Roper swore. "Watch it, Wulff! Whattaya think—"

"*You* watch it." The pack leader was on his feet, towering over the seated Backer. "And *you* watch it, Mister Hamburger-face God-shouter. I've had a gut-full of your sweet Jesus."

Backer didn't move. "Why don't you try Him, Wulff?"

The flames danced and crackled while Wulff moved his lips. The riders watched in silence.

Then with a kick to the shoulder that didn't quite knock Backer over, Wulff howled, "Because it was the Devil who gave me what I wanted!" Then he was gone, out of the firelight, into the trees, taking Shannon with him.

The girl looked over her shoulder at Backer, as if to say something. Then her head jerked forward as Wulff snapped her arm, pulling her along.

"Death just ain't a whole lot to want, Wulff," replied Backer.

He lingered for a time. The party grew wilder.

"You're crazy, Backer," Roper said at last, walking alongside Clint as the rider made his way back to where the Harley leaned on its kickstand.

Backer swung aboard. "Crazier 'n you or them?"

Roper grinned.

"I'm staying the night—what's left of it—at that little bit of a motel above the town. The one from last year?"

Roper nodded, an odd look in his sleepy eyes. "String of cabins in the middle of no place particular?"

"Yeah. Anybody wants me, that's where I'll be." As the bike started to climb, he waved over his shoulder without looking back.

"I wonder if you know where you really are, Clint," Roper mumbled into the wind. "For your sake I hope so . . . I surely do."

Shivering slightly, he went back through the night to the fire's heat.

———

Backer sat on the bunk, stripped to his jeans. Stars burnt tiny holes in the night sky outside his dirty window. As far as he could tell, his was the only occupied cabin of the six scattered under the pines.

"If only—" he said, tossing a boot into the corner, "—there was some way to show 'em. They took me 'n Colt in when nobody else would give us the time of night."

He flopped back on the bed, still in his jeans. "If only I could make 'em see what You did . . ."

He did not know how long it was before the thin panel of the bungalow door began bulging inward under repeated hammer blows.

"Yeah, yeah . . . okay, okay." The door bounced open on a wall of flesh filling the door frame.

"You got some time, or is you sleepy?" Godzilla asked.

"Both. C'mon in."

The bedsprings creaked. "Sometimes, like when we done that peyote, I can *see*, y' know, that there's more than just this here. But then I gets straight, an' there's nothin' left but this big ol' Okie an' me inside him."

"'Cause dope just sets you up to knock you down." Backer held up his battered Bible, once taken from the debris of a bookstore, long since paid for. "This tells you how it works, and it doesn't wear off in the morning. It says God made you and loves you."

Godzilla gave his high-pitched chuckle. "He got some peculiar designs."

"He . . . appreciates you, dig?"

"You keep layin' down that rap."

"*He* keeps doin' it."

"No offense, but you Backers always been crazier 'n a hound in a henhouse. How can I be sure?"

"Ask Him."

The door rattled again, and when it opened on the cold mountain air Roper snarled, "What's he doing here?"

Before Godzilla could reply, Backer said, "He wants to rap about Christ."

After a second's pause Roper entered, then folded himself on the floor like a cat.

"Me too."

Sitting on the bed, Backer flipped open the Book. "It's just the easiest thing—"

Like curls of smoke, clouds drifted over the moon as the three riders talked. At last Godzilla heaved himself to his feet. "Y' all make it sound real good, but that last peyote trip was good too."

"God'll get you there, Godz. 'Holy dope' ain't gonna."

"There's just one way with you, ain't there?"

Backer dropped the Bible onto the bed as Roper uncoiled himself and drifted to the door.

"I guess I'd just hafta see it to believe it."

"It's all real, Rope."

Roper went through the door. A blast of cold air sent goose bumps rising over Backer's bare chest. "I just hope you can hold on to it. But anyway, thanks, Backer. I think I owe you."

Backer smiled. "I'll put it on your tab."

———

At the party deep in the pines, Wulff suddenly thrust Shannon away.

"S' no good!" he snarled, thrusting up a hand and tearing a living tree limb loose with a snap. "It's all lies, and we're gonna show him."

"Honey?" Shannon stumbled through the pines after Wulff as he thrashed through the brush and back to the center of camp. Muttering, he poked up the fire with the branch and then tossed it into the blaze.

By its flickering light he moved through the revelers, pulling them to their feet, tossing them toward the flame. "Spyder! Porky! Deacon! C'mon, you guys, roust it!"

A fistful of riders clustered around their leader.

"You gonna let that goody-two-boots God steal Backer from us?"

There was rumbled dissent.

"What runs with the pack stays with the pack. Shannon, you always had a yen for that ugly red-eyed Scout."

He put his hand on her throat, cutting off her protest.

"Skip the lies . . . I seen it. Tonight you can get him, you little silver-haired witch, and we get back our own."

More Wolves were jostling about now.

"Lissen . . . Cut your engines a ways back in the trees. Shannon will wake up our little Jesus her own special way."

He paused to chuckle at the strategy, the corners of his lip dropping to expose his canines. "Then we bust in, catch him with his pants down, and show him what his holy-roly stuff's worth when push comes to love."

Shannon shook her head, a flare of fright in her gray eyes. "No, Wulff, don't make me . . . He's different."

"He's a man. Backer will fall like a sack full of rocks. I know my Scout. Only reason he's kept his hand off you is 'cause he's my best friend." He shoved her away from the fire. "Get the van. This'll be entertaining."

———

Unable to sleep, Backer padded to the window and tugged down the thin shade. It snapped back up, letting in the starlight. With a sigh he dropped to the side of the bed, still in his jeans, crossed his hands, and prayed like a little child.

"They helped me once, Lord. They were my friends. Please, whatever it takes, let 'em see *You*, not me."

His words seemed to bounce off the mirror of the cheap bureau, but something else mingled in the echo.

Are you willing?

"Whatever it takes."

Can you do what I did?

"I'm only me. But I love these guys."

I will teach you how to love.

Perhaps he actually heard none of this, for he had rolled onto the bunk and his breathing was regular. Perhaps he only dreamed.

Warm hands were on his bare chest. His eyes snapped open. Shannon was leaning over him, her hair white in the moonlight, dangling softly across his shoulders.

"Clint . . ." She raised her head, and her hair whisked over his throat.

He looked into her gray eyes.

Her hands froze.

"Don't," she said. "Please don't look at me like that."

She pulled away, stumbled, fell to her knees against the bunk.

"It was a mistake . . . I'm sorry."

He rolled over, then snapped on the dim bedside light.

"You're not even Clint Backer anymore."

"I will be." He sat up.

"You talk crazy too."

"I'm gonna be the guy I was supposed to be . . . From my DNA on up. I'm through getting worked over by every misfit that takes a notion." He paused. "From my Ma to Wulff. They got their own baggage, and maybe I can help 'em give it up, but I ain't carrying it anymore."

"What *are* you?" She drew her hand across her mouth.

"What are *you?*"

"No more games . . . please. I think I'm gonna scream."

"Don't scream. Tell me *who* you are, Shannon."

"Nobody in particular. Shannon Polanski . . . Wulff's old lady."

Rolling off the bed, he came to rest on his knees beside her. "Lady, you are worth dying for and God wants to forgive you and make you special through His love."

"Clint, I got nothing much to live for, let alone . . . the other. Who in the name of God would die for a twenty-six-year-old high-school dropout named Shannon Polanski?"

"You stop whining, chick . . . Listen up and I'll tell you." He took her hands, his rust-colored eyes looking into her wide gray ones, and began.

———

Two blows and the door split at the frame and slammed open. Wulff pushed through, and a half-dozen riders behind him spilled into the little room.

"So the mighty Scout has feet of clay right up to the neck!" he shouted flipping on the overhead light. "'Greater love hath no man than he lays down the chick of his—'"

The coarse babble dried up. Backer and Shannon looked up from where they still knelt at the bedside, hands clasped in prayer, Clint's black Bible from a long-ago night in Boulder open on the bed.

"I . . . did something tonight, Wulff," Shannon burst out. Not what you think. Clint—he showed me a new way. I'm gonna be different—"

Savagely Wulff struck her. She tumbled against the nightstand. The table and lamp toppled onto her.

"My woman too! You thiever—" Droplets of saliva sprayed out from his contorted mouth as he pounced on Backer, his white fingers twisted into claws.

"Shannon!" Backer was up, his leg darting out, two

hundred pounds of healthy muscle reflex digging into Wulff's midsection.

Wulff sailed backward, then slammed into Porky and Spyder. All three slammed out the door, hit the ground, and skidded twenty feet through the dirt.

Stunned silence.

Like scalded cats, the other riders pulled away from Backer.

Arms held high and circling, Clint tilted a little to the side, his legs wide apart and lightly balanced in front of the crumpled girl. His lips trembled.

His own words hung in the air. *Some way to show them.*

"Shannon?" he whispered, listening to the scrabbling as Wulff dragged himself through the mud to the porch and pulled himself to his feet.

But then he understood. It was just him they wanted, had to have . . . the one who escaped.

Slowly he forced himself to lower his hands to his sides.

"Wulff," he began urgently, "so long we've been friends and . . . we always just took each other the way we were. I know I hurt you—"

With an animal cry Wulff launched himself from the doorway. He hit Backer, and the two of them slammed into the bureau. The mirror shattered. They fell to the floor, rolled.

Many hands dragged Backer to his feet, shoved him up against the wall. He saw Wulff raise his hands, fingers curling into fists, level with Backer's face.

"I'm gonna snuff you."

"I love you."

A fist drove into his lips. Two teeth crumpled and

were gone. His nose broke, blood spattering as it crunched sideways against his cheek.

They hit him again.

And again.

And again.

Dimly, from the floor, he heard Wulff say, "Carry him to the van. We'll finish this at the camp. Spyder, make your hook useful—grab his keys. Take the bike. Don't leave nothin'."

First the ceiling came toward him and then the far-away blackness of the night sky. As the van doors slammed, shutting off the night, Wulff's word's carried back.

"When we get there, leave the keys in the Harley. He's not gonna need it ever again."

15

OUTSIDE THE CAMP

In an Alexander house guest room, Dawn awoke screaming.

Blind, she did not reach for the light switch, but sat trembling as the breeze from the open window snapped at the red-and-white checked curtains.

Anna Alexander came in, throwing a yellow silk kimono over her friend's shoulders. "Child, what is it?"

"Clint," Dawn said, still half-asleep.

"You were dreaming."

Dawn's eye's flicked wide, and Mrs. Alexander knew she was seeing, but in a manner Anna could not comprehend.

"He's still in Central City, I suppose. Do you want me to call Eagle's Wing to see if Niklhas has heard anything?"

Dawn shook her head.

"Then there's nothing for us to do but pray."

"Yes." Dawn slipped from under the comforter.

Withdrawing a light yellow robe from the closet, Mrs. Alexander put it across the girl's shoulders. Without another word the two women knelt at the bedside beneath the open window.

————

Through the long ride, Backer was dimly aware of a girl's sobbing.

Shannon, he tried to say, *not time for weeping anymore.* Wanting to say something to comfort the girl, he was frustrated by the sound of someone groaning. After a while, he realized the groans were his.

And then they were there—down the slope and into the dusty street of the old camp. The van pulled up not far from the bonfire. Most of the crowd was still there, dancing and drinking around the dimming blaze.

The van doors swung open. He was pitched out into the street.

"Why'd he stop fighting?"

"You see him hit Wulff? I ain't never seen anybody do him like that."

"I ain't ever seen Wulff crazy like that."

"But why'd Backer stop? It looked like—" The speaker lowered his voice. "—looked like Backer coulda took him."

Though he was on his back and his eyes were nearly swollen shut, Backer looked up. He saw a wall of fire as a backdrop, and a pulsating crowd around him: men with devil horns, Frankenstein monsters, girls in seductive gowns, riders in their leathers with the snarling wolf's-head everywhere.

Someone kicked his already-broken rib.

He groaned.

"Wherezzat bullhorn?" Wulff was over him, his black hair flickering over his large white face.

Deacon ducked inside another van and tossed the bullhorn to the leader. Wulff snatched it out of the air, snapped it, on and rasped into the tube, "Here's the traitor. He lied to us, and he left us. Nobody does that to the pack."

There were cries of drunken anger.

"He ain't got nothin', and you all know it."

Spyder shook his head. "But how come he let you beat him, Wulff? He didn't look scared."

"He kept sayin'," Porky shook his head, "that he loved you."

"He's crazy! He's a liar! You saw where it got him!"

"It got me here." They all heard Backer's croak from where he lay crumpled.

"And he didn't *let* me beat him! It was justice! . . . The strong over the weak!"

There were murmurs from the crowd, but not the enthusiastic demand for blood Wulff had anticipated.

Stooping, his fingers dug into Backer's hair, he hissed, "Tell 'em you lost or I'll finish fryin' your head." With hysterical strength he dragged Backer by the roots of his hair to the flame.

Backer's scalp began to blister. The smell of charred hair wafted through the mountain night.

Not the fire again. God, please, not the fire.

"I'll . . . tell 'em," he managed to say through lips three times their normal size.

"You tell 'em I'm stronger. You tell 'em the truth or you'll burn," Wulff threatened in his ear as he hauled him upright.

Backer swayed, supported by Deacon and Spyder. Blood ran down his face and over his bare chest in rivulets. Stones cut into his naked soles.

The bullhorn was thrust at his purple lips.

"He's gonna tell you the truth!" Wulff screamed, and his normally whispery voice carried over the camp.

The crowd of Halloween witches, demons, beasts, ballerinas, and bikers waited while Clint swallowed, struggling to work his tongue.

The fire popped.

"Wolves!" he began, and the electronic croak of the bullhorn emphasized the lisp as he tried to deal with the missing front teeth. "Long-time old-time friends . . ."

Somebody hooted.

"Me, my brother Colt . . . we had nothin' once. And you guys . . . you took us in. We stuck together. We were family."

Wulff nodded his approval.

"But families die. Colt died. For nothing. He had nothing. I thought—he thought—he could deal with that nothing—"

They were beginning to growl, and Wulff tried to yank the bullhorn away. Backer's hand swung up, held Wulff's wrist with strength that should not have been there.

"Nothingness hurts. It burns worse than the flames. And death isn't just nothing. It's pain!"

Wulff was fighting for the amplifier now, but Backer desperately held on, his knees sagging. The struggle brought other riders surging forward.

"There is something! Someone! He not only takes you in, He makes you somebody you don't have to be ashamed of anymore, down inside, deep. It was the Enemy screwed life up so bad. Christ wants us! Wants to get us through! Make things right for us! We're family! Us bikers and dopeheads and screw-ups and everybody! We're all as good as the fat cats to Him! He loves us! *He wants us Home!*"

A fist tore the words from his mouth as his head bounced back and his body sagged. He fell.

"All right!" Wulff screamed. "It's good enough for your boss, it's good enough for you!" He thrust an arm outward at the darkness, toward the hilltop where The Lynching Tree with its blazing pumpkin victim still twisted against the moon.

"Crucify him!"

Raised up and carried hand over hand, they took him up the hill. He was held up to face the suspended dummy.

Deacon and Spyder clambered up the boxes, then hauled themselves to the splintered treetop. Clinging to the cross-bar formed by the opposing branches, Deacon drew a K-bar from his boot and with its blade cut through the hangman's knot that held the effigy.

The dummy toppled to the ground, and the crowd cheered, the pumpkin head bouncing as the light in its eye sockets wavered and died.

Thrust up over the scaffold of debris, Backer's arms were clutched by Deacon and Spyder, who dragged him to the pinnacle nine feet above the mob.

"Here!" Porky had sliced the dummy's death rope into pieces, and he flung them to Deacon, who snagged them deftly and tossed a strand to Spyder. They wrapped Backer's wrists against the branches. Spyder's hook left bloody trails down Backer's arm.

He dangled from the tree, bare feet scraping the bark.

Old ore-track ties had been turned into torches, and

by their light Backer saw a fist raise up, clutching a seven-inch track spike, red with rust.

And then he saw two more.

"Love of God, Wulff, no! Please!" Shannon shouted, reaching for the spike.

Wulff pushed her away. They handed him an old miner's sledgehammer, ancient as the spikes, ancient as their business.

At the top of the tree Deacon grabbed the fingers of Backer's right hand, pried them apart.

Wulff clambered over boxes and barrels, wobbled, found his balance, and faced Backer, holding the heavy hammer in both hands.

"Good-bye, old friend." Wulff pulled the sledge back over his left shoulder.

From up above, Deacon placed the point of the rusty spike on Backer's opened palm.

"I know where I'm goin'!" Backer cried out over their heads. "You got no place left to go but Hell!"

"We're already there." Wulff started to bring the hammer forward.

———

Across town from the bedroom where Dawn and Mrs. Alexander knelt praying, lights burned late in the windows of the Eagle's Wing library.

All around the conference table, kneeling at the chairs and standing in groups, members of the fellowship prayed.

"How long?" Chavez wondered when Niklhas informed him of the vigil.

"As long as we need to."

"How will we know?"

"Some of us will know."

So they prayed, and Halloween's darkness melted into the dawn of All Saints' Day. Only a few remained in the library through the night, but Niklhas stayed at the table's head. His thick hands were clasped, and sweat ran down his face.

In the woman's wing Nora, in her bedroom darkness, stood alone at the window, lips moving.

Hands resting on the old globe, Darcey stared out the window onto Logan Street, his thin face pulled tight, eyes burning as the night began to end.

━━━━━

From somewhere a wave, a ripple of strength, seemed to come over the hill and wash over Backer as he hung from the cross. Perhaps it was only the peace that sometimes accompanies the certainty of death, when all struggling ceases.

Hanging from the tree by his wrists, Backer looked into Wulff's eyes. "Christ does love you," he said as Wulff hesitated. "And I love you."

He knew it was true as he spoke it, and he closed his eyes to die.

"Give the Man my regards," Wulff managed to say, "'cause you'll be right up." The hammer swung.

Whhhaaaackkk! The sound shrieked, then vibrated in the night.

It was the meaty smack of stricken flesh as the old

sledge handle collided—not with Backer, but with Godzilla's outstretched palms.

Arrested in its trajectory, the wooden handle quivered and snapped, and the mallet head toppled with a crash into the crates beneath it.

Godzilla, precariously straddling the two barrels that groaned beneath his bulk, gripped the thick handle in both fists.

"Nobody," he enunciated carefully, "is nailin' nobody to nothin'."

"You stupid bag of guts!" Wulff dived for the handle. "We'll kill you too!"

The handle blurred downward, struck hard. Yelping, Wulff drew back a shattered right hand, nursed it against his chest.

"You guys is the stupids." Godzilla kept his balance astride the barrels. "This guy comes sayin' he's got somethin' and look at cha . . . You so scared, you gonna just plumb waste a man that only wants to show you somethin' better than what you got." He spat tobacco. "Which, if you was to ask me, and nobody ever does, just don't make a whole lotta sense."

Snarling, Wulff tried to scramble up the pile of debris. "You and that fool on the tree against us all. There's still just two of you."

"Three." Roper tossed Deacon, still gripping the spike, off the tree.

Deacon skidded down the stack of crates and rammed into Wulff. They both fell to the ground.

"Take 'em." Wulff pushed away Deacon and struggled to his knees. "Kill 'em. Burn 'em."

"You gonna have a time of it." Godzilla lowered his head and raised the sledge handle.

"A real hard time." Roper's switchblade *snickked* open as he hopped to the ground, then kicked a box from his path. Before Wulff could make it off his knees, Roper's blade pushed under his jaw.

"No offense, Wulff . . ." Godzilla looked down at him. ". . . but I don't think you're leader anymore. S' nothin' personal. You just too empty."

Hesitantly the Wolves moved forward.

The wave surged then, flowing out from Eagle's Wing and the Alexander house and perhaps from places entirely different. Backer felt something pour through him, fill him, push his aching right arm outward, straining against its bonds. The muscles in his shoulder swelled.

The old strand of mining camp rope split, and his right hand burst loose. With unnatural speed he twisted as he fell, grasping the branch that still held his left wrist.

His grip held. Taking his bound forearm in the fingers of his free hand, with an effort that should have made his fractured ribs scream, he pulled.

The old branch, lightning-blasted and riddled with decay, cracked away from the tree.

Backer disappeared with a crash into the stack of scavenged cargo at the base of the trunk.

Wulff tried to regain his feet, but Roper's knife pricked his throat, drawing blood.

Godzilla jumped from the collapsing platform to stand beside Roper.

Up out of the center of the wreckage Backer suddenly stood. He flung aside a barrel and pushed through the debris, the thick end of The Lynching Tree branch still dangling from the loop around his left wrist.

"No . . ." Backer's right hand stopped the blade, and

his other pushed down the sledge, the branch below his wrist swinging.

"There ain't but the one way with you, is there?" snarled Roper, lowering the knife.

"There's only that One Way."

Backer stepped between Roper and Godzilla and stood over the crouching leader.

"It's over, Wulff."

Drying blood etched trails down Backer's face and dripped onto his chest. His swollen eyes were almost closed, his nose was pushed against his cheek, and when he drew thick lips back from his missing teeth his words were blurred.

"My death wouldn't have changed anything. The only death that counted happened long ago, and what happened after is still happening. But it's not too late maybe for you to come over to the winning side."

Wulff shuffled backwards through the dirt on his knees. Fingers splayed, he gripped Spyder's vest and hauled himself upright.

"Take him!" he cried, eyes wide.

Spyder looked away, backed up.

"They left the family!" Saliva ran down his chin. He tugged at Deacon. "Kill them! Kill them for Poppa!"

Reaching up, Deacon slowly unfastened Wulff's claw-like hand from his jacket. "I think it's time," he said, "to go . . . someplace else."

He left Wulff there, still pleading, and walked past Backer. His eyes flickered over him the briefest instant. Then he was gone in the waning darkness, down the slope to the camp. A few moments later the sound of his chopper floated over the hill as he took the trail out the opposite end of camp.

"Porky! Chico!"

No recognition was given to the leader as one by one the riders filed past Backer, who stood with his hands at his sides, the thick black branch dangling from his left wrist, his streaked body turning orange-red in the first rays of dawn.

"Something . . ." Porky said to him, pausing a moment, "there's definitely something . . ." Then he shrugged and was gone in the mob.

Even Roper and Godzilla vanished, as if they had been no more than evening campfire smoke fading with first light. Only Shannon remained, slumped at the foot of the hanging tree, her soft sobs carried away by the wind.

"I lost," Wulff said from the edge of the hill, "this time. But there's plenty of others out there. Rejects, castoffs. Families don't want 'em. Churches don't want 'em."

He paused for breath, and his voice was his and yet other than his. "They're mine. You try and take them, and next time I *will* kill you."

"It's been tried," answered Backer, and his voice was his and more than his. "You lost the war two thousand years ago."

Then Wulff was gone, stumbling down the hill.

At the sound of engines, Backer turned into the rising sun. Squinting against the glare, he saw Roper and Godzilla returning on their bikes.

"I was wrong," Roper said. "You *can* hang on to what you found. Can you ever."

"He hangs on to me."

"Yeah. I got to think." He lifted his arm, gave the biker's clenched-fist salute, and jerked his machine around.

Backer returned the salute, extending his index finger to transform it into the One Way sign.

Godzilla only smiled, reaching up to gently tip his helmet. Then he gunned his Harley, following Roper down the hill, away from the tree, in the opposite direction from that taken by the Wolves.

At the moment they departed, the tide washing over Backer departed. He sank to his knees like a marionette with the strings cut.

He tried to make his way over to Shannon. Searing tentacles of pain from his ribs sent him pitching forward again, and he began to drag himself across the ground.

Then Shannon was helping him, assisting him to his feet while his ribs screamed.

"The middle of nowhere—" she was crying, her arms around his crusted shoulders as he hobbled forward. "You can't—"

"Get me to my bike," he said, or tried to say. "I know a medic."

"You can't drive, or even hang on." They were slipping down the hill.

"You'll drive, I'll hang on . . . All the way. I know how to do that."

———

The thunder woke Kobol. He grabbed the bedside clock, stared, then slapped it down. It fell off the nightstand.

The rumble became a slamming. He blinked. There was thudding at the door.

Grumbling, he swung his legs off the side of the bed, staggered up, and wrapped a too-short purple robe around him.

The dog was barking now, and he tripped over it as he padded to the front door.

"Intrusion, close it up!" He swung wide the door.

The girl's long white-silver hair, ironed straight in the fashion of the times, brushed the shoulders of a low-cut black gown.

"Morticia, right?" He yawned. "From 'The Addams Family.' Halloween's over, lady."

"He said you were his friend." Kobol became aware of her puffy eyes and tear-stained face.

"He said you were a medic."

"A medic?" Then, over her shoulder he saw Backer's Harley in its old familiar spot. There was a bundle of red rags spread across the handlebars and seat.

Down the steps, across the yard . . . Kobol picked up the rider as if he were no more than a child.

"In the Mekong Delta, boy, I saw guys killed in firefights that looked better 'n you do."

"I fought the fire," Backer mumbled before his head dropped back, slack.

"And this time I bet our side won." Kobol's hand pressed the rider's face to his chest as he carried him up the steps and into the house, the girl following.

THE ROAD

He was carrying the next-to-last load down the stairs. Most of what he owned had been given away, the small remainder now strapped to his Harley.

"Slow down," Chavez rasped. "The bandages only been off two weeks."

Standing on the old walnut staircase at Eagle's Wing, Backer paused long enough to shake his head.

Surgery had put most of his pieces back in place, though the network of white burn tissue would always stretch across his right cheek, and the hump at the bridge of his reset nose was larger, which, Niklhas had observed, only increased his resemblance to the eagle engraved out front.

"More like a gargoyle on that cathedral downtown," Chavez had commented, earning one of Backer's rare smiles, revealing the gap between his new front teeth.

"You really think you have to go?" asked Niklhas now.

Bouncing down the rest of the stairs, Backer replied, "After they finally sprung me from the hospital, I stuck

around 'til Christmas to play best man at your wedding."
He headed for the front door. "Then I waited through
New Year's Day, so I could clean up from you guys on the
bowl games. Now it's time."

Standing on the porch, Nora blocked his path.

"You can't. Since Mrs. Alexander's newspaper stories
have been coming out, you're a public figure."

"People ask for you." Shannon wiped her hands on
her apron. "You owe them."

"That's why I'm going." Hands full, he tried to move
past the girls and out the door.

Not budging an inch, the six-foot Nora insisted, "Just
yesterday there were a couple of bikers asking about you."

"And several of Nora's old . . . associates want to talk
to you," Shannon put in.

"Yeah." Sighing, Backer put down his load, reached
over, picked up Nora, and moved her aside.

"Hey, you ape!"

"So sorry, Big Blonde, but you and Shannon keep this
household running now. What comes up, you can handle,
or pass up the line."

From the second floor Darcey's angry voice floated
down. He was leaning against the railing, knuckles white
on the balustrade. "What about me? What about us?"

"With the transfer to D.U., you can make the fall
semester, stay here at Eagle's Wing. Plenty of room out
back for your workshop." Backer made his way out the
door, strapped a load on his Harley, and bounded up the
stairs again. "With you and your mom getting on, she can
advise you on setting up in business. You'll be self-support-
ing by Easter."

As the last load was brought down, Dawn came to
him.

"Clint, there's something I'd like you to see."

He followed her to a small outbuilding that had once been a potting shed. The bust she had labored over stood on a bench, cloth-covered.

"It's done . . . All by touch. People say it's pretty good."

She flicked off the cloth.

Backer swallowed. It was his likeness, yet it wasn't. The burns were absent, but the damage his face had endured that night outside the camp was there: swollen eyes, split lips, shattered nose, even the missing teeth.

"How could you?" he asked.

"In the hospital, this last time, remember? When the bandages were off, I touched your poor face . . . and Nik described you."

The head was encircled by a crown of thorns.

"That's not Peter," he said, "it's Christ."

"Yes . . . the suffering servant. What do you think?"

He covered it with the cloth. "A great career lies ahead of you, if only you stop being influenced by Goya and itinerant bikers."

"Oh, Clint—" She kissed him.

Niklhas was in the doorway. "A sucker for anyone who admires her art," he said. Then, "What about the Foundation vice president slot?"

Backer stalked through the house for the final time. "Chavez."

"Uh-uh, home boy." Chavez, in the front hall, shook his head. "I don't like neckties."

"Acting veep then. Until Darcey's old enough."

Niklhas put a hand on the rider's arm, turned him as he was going out into the bright sunshine.

"Two questions before you fade off into the smog."

They were beside the motorcycle now. Backer swung aboard. "The first?"

"When you comin' back, Smart Guy?"

Backer kicked the starter. "Charter says you got a yearly meeting. If I'm still official veep, then I guess I should attend. 'Sides, ter Horst will be done clambering over his Mid-East ruins by then. I want to hear him tell us how he unearthed ancient scrolls proving the lost tribes of Israel were all Dutchmen."

Niklhas laughed softly.

"And the second question?" Backer glanced up at Eagle's Wing. Shannon and Nora stood on the porch. Dawn was by the open gate. Darcey stared down from the library window. Chavez knelt on the lawn.

"Why?"

Backer sighed. "They're out there—the rest of the Wolves, whatever they call themselves now. The homeless, the wanderers, the outlaws. Some of 'em will hear and will come to you. But the rest—they're trapped in pits of darkness, and we got the Light. I can go where you never could. That's what I have to do. Maybe that's what I was born for."

He revved his machine.

"What about your schooling?"

Backer turned the wheel toward the street. "There are other schools. I got close to a 4.0 average and some good recommendations." He looked up at Niklhas. "What Anna would call the right stuff for a resumé. For that matter, not all correspondence schools are diploma mills."

He pushed the bike forward. "I socked away some cash. When it runs out, I'll work."

Edging into traffic, he glanced back a final time.

"Thank you," he called, and his wave included everyone at the house.

"Thank you," answered Niklhas, putting an arm around Dawn. They climbed back up the steps of Eagle's Wing.

Backer turned left onto Colfax, moving toward Broadway.

As he approached the intersection, the thunder of other machines hit his back.

Glancing in the mirror, he saw a helmet bobbing up and down. The wide face beneath it smiled.

A second rider appeared, raising his fist in a biker's salute, and then the index finger jutted skyward, making the One Way sign.

Grinning into his mirror, Backer returned the salute.

Roper and Godzilla followed his growling Harley as he glided toward the Interstate.